WARDENCLYFFE

JournalStone books may be ordered through booksellers or by contacting:

JournalStone
www.journalstone.com

ISBN: 978-1-947654-59-4 (sc)
ISBN: 978-1-947654-60-0 (ebook)

JournalStone rev. date: December 14, 2018

Library of Congress Control Number: 2018957155

Printed in the United States of America

Cover Art & Design: Mihai Costea
Interior Layout: Jess Landry

Edited by Vincenzo Bilof
Proofread by Sean Leonard

ALSO BY F. PAUL WILSON

Repairman Jack*
The Tomb
Legacies
Conspiracies
All the Rage
Hosts
The Haunted Air
Gateways
Crisscross
Infernal
Harbingers
Bloodline
By the Sword
Ground Zero
Fatal Error
The Dark at the End
Nightworld
Quick Fixes Tales of Repairman Jack

The Teen Trilogy*
Jack: Secret Histories
Jack: Secret Circles
Jack: Secret Vengeance

The Early Years Trilogy*
Cold City
Dark City
Fear City

The Adversary Cycle*
The Keep
The Tomb
The Touch
Reborn
Reprisal
Nightworld

Omnibus Editions
The Complete LaNague
Calling Dr. Death (3 medical thrillers)
Ephemerata

The LaNague Federation
Healer
Wheels Within Wheels
An Enemy of the State
Dydeetown World
The Tery

Other Novels
*Black Wind**
*Sibs**
The Select
Virgin
Implant
Deep as the Marrow
Mirage (with Matthew J. Costello)
Nightkill (with Steven Spruill)
Masque (with Matthew J. Costello)
Sims
*The Fifth Harmonic**
Midnight Mass
The Proteus Cure (with Tracy L. Carbone)
A Necessary End (with Sarah Pinborough)

The ICE Trilogy
*Panacea**
*The God Gene**
*The Void Protocol**

The Nocturnia Chronicles
(with Thomas F. Monteleone)
Definitely Not Kansas
Family Secrets
The Silent Ones

Short Fiction
Soft & Others
The Barrens and Others
Aftershock and Others
The Christmas Thingy
*The Peabody-Ozymandias Traveling Circus &
Oddity Emporium**
*Quick Fixes Tales of Repairman Jack**
Sex Slaves of the Dragon Tong

Editor
Freak Show
Diagnosis: Terminal
The Hogben Chronicles (with Pierce Watters)

* see "The Secret History of the
World" (page 141)

WARDENCLYFFE

F. PAUL WILSON

JOURNALSTONE
YOUR LINK TO ARTIST TALENT

To
Eugene Johnson

Thanks for the spark.

OCTOBER 12, 1937

As I watched for him to exit the New Yorker, I wondered if he still blamed himself for all those deaths in San Francisco.

I hadn't wanted to call up from the front desk or be associated with him in any way—for both our sakes. So I loitered outside the hotel where he'd lived for the past three years and waited, leaning against an Eighth Avenue lamppost and reading the *Herald Tribune*.

None of the news was good. What the world was calling the Great Depression had seemed to be easing last year, but government "adjustments" had ratcheted unemployment back up to 17 percent, creating an Even Greater Depression. The international scene looked worse. As a former British citizen, I was distressed by the news that the Duke and Duchess of Windsor had boarded a train in Paris for a trip to Nazi Germany. The Nazis repulsed me as much as I would repulse them.

And then a story about the Lindberghs making their second visit to the Nazis. What was *wrong* with these people?

The stories and their implications absorbed me to the point where I almost missed him. I might have missed him anyway, considering how he'd changed.

Well, what did I expect? Three decades had passed. The twentieth century was still in its infancy when we'd last stood face to face. Of course I'd seen him on the cover of *Time* in celebration of his seventy-fifth birthday. Even then he'd looked quite different from the man I'd known, though he'd still sported that thick mustache and much of his hair had retained its dark color.

But this gaunt, sunken-cheeked, white-haired gent with the clean-shaven face…could it really be? He wore a dark gray three-piece suit, a white shirt, and a black tie. He used to wear spats when I knew him, but not today. Probably not for a long time. He'd always liked to stay in style and spats were long passé. He glanced at me with no sign of recognition, but I knew those dark eyes and that strong nose.

He walked with a limp and used a cane, and that made me sad. But again, what did I expect? The man was eighty-one after all.

The looming tower of the Empire State Building jutted into the sky ahead as I followed him two blocks west on 34th Street. Along the way we passed a sad array of shabby men holding signs begging for jobs. I counted myself so lucky to still have one. I worked for Chicago and the city needed electricity to light its offices and run the trains around the Loop. As an electrical engineer, I'd been kept on while so many others had been let go. My heart went out to all of them.

The man ahead of me seemed oblivious. Just as he'd been oblivious all those years ago to the doom he'd allowed into this world. I'd managed to seal off those memories…the horror gushing from the ground and climbing toward the stars…but seeing him again in the flesh caused a stirring behind the walls.

He turned downtown on Sixth Avenue; after one block he angled between a pair of granite columns topped with black iron eagles and entered a tiny, roughly triangular park. Wrought iron rails fenced it off from the sidewalks. A large statue of a seated man—Horace Greeley, according to the plaque—dominated the center, so I imagined the space carried his name. I trailed him to an empty bench where he pulled out a bag of seed and began feeding the pigeons.

After a moment's hesitation, I settled next to him. "Nikola Tesla, I presume?"

He gave me a quick up and down. "You presume correctly." His voice had aged too, raspy now, but his Serbian accent remained the same. "I am not giving interviews today."

"Don't you recognize me?"

He looked again, giving me a long squint, then shook his head. "Sorry, I cannot say that I do."

"It's Charles…Charles Atkinson."

A longer squint, and then a look of concern. "Charles! Is that really you?"

"Really me."

"I didn't recognize you. You…you have a mustache! You could never grow one!"

I smoothed the dark silky strands along my upper lip. I was perhaps inordinately proud of the growth.

"I was a much younger man back then—just barely twenty-five, remember? I'm middle fifties now."

A look of alarm flattened his features. He lowered his voice. "But why are you here? Is it about…you know?"

I assumed he was referring to that night in 1906, the details of which we'd sworn to carry to our graves.

"No-no," I said quickly. "Nothing like that."

"You shouldn't be here. Please don't look around when I say this, but I am being watched."

It took every fiber of my will not to do just that. "Are you sure?"

"It's been going on for years. They haven't contacted you?"

I had no idea whom he meant. "No one's contacted me. I'm here from Chicago on business."

His expression relaxed. "Then do not trouble yourself."

"Why would the government contact me?"

"It is nothing." His sudden smile looked forced. "Here on business, you say? Who do you work for?"

I'd been dreading this question. "Don't be angry: Commonwealth Edison."

He looked away and shook his head. "That name remains everywhere. Just last year New York Edison changed its name—to *Consolidated* Edison. Edison, Edison, Edison! He's long dead and yet all these companies make millions upon millions under his name using *my* current!"

I laid a gentle hand on his shoulder—he was all bone beneath the fabric—and let him stew a moment. Finally he reached up and patted my hand.

"You are an electrical engineer, Charles. I realize it is almost impossible to work in your field without being connected to that name. But why Chicago?"

Now we came to the reason I'd sought him out.

"Well, because after you shut down the project, we agreed to separate and keep a low profile. Which is exactly what I did. However, I fear I cannot say the same for you."

"I tried," he said. "Oh, how I tried. I declared bankruptcy and feigned a nervous breakdown after Wardenclyffe. I even moved to Chicago myself for a year—with no idea you were there—but I hated it. I thought I'd succeeded in finding obscurity when they dragged me out to receive the Edison Medal, of all things." His mouth twisted as though he'd bitten into something rotten. "The *Edison* Medal."

Yes. How that must have rankled.

I reminded him, "It's perhaps the highest honor in our field."

"I know, I know. I would have seemed petty had I refused it. But after that, the spotlight kept falling on me. So I decided to hide in plain sight."

"I don't see how saying you'd been contacted by beings from space and talking of death rays and such is hiding. And thought cameras, maestro? *Thought* cameras?"

He started to laugh but it cut off as he winced and pressed a hand to the side of his chest. "Please don't make me laugh."

This couldn't be good. "What's wrong?"

"A few weeks ago I was struck by a cab crossing the street. My fault entirely. Many bruises and a number of broken ribs."

"Did you see a doctor?" I knew how he felt about doctors.

"Of course not. What were they going to do? Strap my chest? I did that myself."

I could only shake my head. "Same old stubborn Serb."

He got a sly look. "No, not the same, not the same at all. I've seen to it that I'm now the world's best known mad scientist. That's why I publicly obsess on the number three, why I demand eighteen napkins at each meal. One cannot take a man like that seriously." He pounded his fist on his knee to emphasize each word. "Which is just what I want."

"But your legacy—"

"Is quite secure. That won't go away. The electric power that lights all these buildings and moves the subways running beneath our feet—that is mine. I no longer earn a penny from it, but the fact that I invented it cannot be changed. The man named Nikola Tesla made an enormous contribution to human civilization. Using direct current, humanity could not be where it is now. Alternating current got us here. And I invented it."

Well, there he was, chuffed as ever about his accomplishments. I was glad to see his ego had not suffered from all his financial and professional setbacks since last we met. He'd dwindled physically, but two defining facets of his personality—his stubbornness and his self-regard—remained unchanged from our Wardenclyffe days.

"But I have another legacy, do I not," he added with a haunted expression.

I guessed where this was going. "You're not still blaming—?"

"Thousands of lives, Charles. Three thousand of them, all on my conscience."

"Has that anything to do with your mad-scientist charade?"

He leaned back and seemed to deflate. "I fear the day when my mind starts to slip. What if I begin talking about all that happened? The consequences—"

"Will be nil," I said. "What happened is beyond the wildest imagination. Who in their right mind would believe?"

"They would believe Nikola Tesla, the great thinker, the brilliant scientist and inventor."

I nodded, seeing where he was going. "But they won't believe a mad scientist."

"Exactly. But I have a greater fear: What if someone convinces me to change the circuit diagrams back to their original configurations?"

"Why would anyone do that?"

"If they figure out why they were revised."

"You mean these government men you mentioned—*our* government, I assume?" Nazi agents were rumored to be infiltrating the States.

"They seem to be. But there are others. That secret society wants to collect on a debt."

"What debt?"

"The money they advanced me to keep Wardenclyffe going."

That did it. The walls crumbled and the memories came back in a rush, thundering loose and flooding around me.

TESLA READY FOR BUSINESS
HE HAS BOUGHT THE LAND FOR
HIS WIRELESS TELEGRAPHY STA-
TION AND LET THE CONTRACTS
FOR THE BUILDINGS
New-York Tribune
August 7, 1901

1903

I first saw the Wardenclyffe tower from a train—in Connecticut, of all places. In late May, as I recall, we were gaining speed after a stop at New Haven when a young woman pointed out the window and said, "Oh, look. Tesla's added a cap to his tower!"

My ears pricked up at "Tesla." I'd just been awarded my electrical engineering degree from MIT and so the name of the inventor of AC current, the induction coil, the man who harnessed the power of Niagara Falls to light the entire city of Buffalo, had a magical effect on me.

"Tower?" I said, leaping from my seat across the car. "Where?"

"Right there, silly," she said, pointing again and smiling. "Don't tell me you've never seen it before."

At first look I saw only scrub-filled marshland running down to the wharves that edged the gleaming expanse of the Long Island Sound. I was about to ask again when I saw it. There, on the far shore, the New York shore, a tall skeletal structure rose far above the trees.

Squinting I could see how the crisscrossing struts and trusses of the sturdy tapering base resembled the upper section of the Eiffel Tower. They ran up to a flattened dome with copper fittings gleaming in the sun like fiery jewels. The tower reminded me of nothing so much as a long-stemmed mushroom with an amber cap.

"Blimey," I said, "that thing must be almost two-hundred feet tall."

The girl laughed again. "'Blimey'? Are you a Brit?"

Well, at least she hadn't said "Limey," which had been my nickname at MIT. She appeared about my age, with golden hair bunned-up beneath her hat. She wore a dark-red velvet jacket over a high-collared blouse, and a gown of the same material that ran all the way to the floor.

I, on the other hand, was dressed in my best gray suit—my only suit, truth be known—white shirt with a Pembrook celluloid collar, and a maroon tie. I usually wore a derby but had doffed it for the train ride. In defiance of the current fashion, I was clean shaven and kept my brown hair short, especially the sides; a tad cool in the winter, but good for a quick wash-up in the summer.

"Don't be rude, dear," said the older woman beside her in the window seat—her mother, I presumed.

"Native of Manchester," I said with a little bow, "and not rude in the least. To answer your question, this is my first trip to New York in years. So, no, I have not seen it before."

I could tell they both liked me right off. My slight frame and non-threatening baby face had that effect on women. But the tower laid claim to my interest and would not release me. I spotted a pair of empty seats three rows ahead.

"Excuse me, ladies."

I made my way forward and slipped into the window seat where I stared at Tesla's tower. I'd read about it, of course, and at university we'd often had late-night discussions about Tesla and his notions of wireless communication and wireless power.

Wireless communication had become a reality—already two years now since Guglielmo Marconi had sent a transatlantic message consisting of the letter "S" from Cornwall to Newfoundland. Tesla was suing, claiming Marconi had used seventeen of his patents to accomplish the feat. I had no idea whether or not that was true, but I did know we were living in an age of electrical marvels. And I, with a degree in electrical engineering, stood ready to leap into the fray and create my own.

But wireless power seemed an enormous leap. Still, if anyone could make it work, Nikola Tesla was the man.

Wireless power…the concept inflamed my brain. The air above the streets of every modern city had become bird-nest mazes of wires strung from pole to pole and pole to building, running high, low, lengthwise, crosswise, diagonally. And every day the utility companies added more. At the current rate of proliferation, sunlight would soon stop reaching the pavements. But Tesla's project would make all those wires obsolete. City dwellers could look up and see the sky again.

I stared at that tower, obviously still under construction. Something about its shape, its height, its glinting mushroom cap. So tall, so…defiant. Like a fist raised in challenge to all the doubters. Something about it shouted to my brain.

I am the future, it said. *The future is here. Come build the future with me.*

But I was too sensible for that. I had a plan and it did not include Nikola Tesla.

This trip to New York was for an interview at General Electric's corporate headquarters. They wanted a look at this brand new electrical engineer who had graduated near the top of his class at MIT. I knew they would hire me. Truly, how could they not? I was smart, creative, and got along with everyone.

I'd done my research. General Electric was a company with a future. When Dow and Jones assembled their Industrial Average, they began by choosing twelve companies that best represented American industry. General Electric was one of those twelve. A company destined for growth, and I could grow with it. My future was assured and I was delirious with the possibilities.

But that tower…that tower jutting from the horizon. It called to me.

And if the great Nikola Tesla proved his theory…if he indeed began to send power wirelessly around the globe, then every other electrical company was in trouble.

The tenements of east New Haven soon blocked my view of the tower but I remained at the window, staring out, thinking.

I had my appointment with GE and I would keep it. But I would also make the trek out to the north shore of Long Island to visit Wardenclyffe.

Just for a look.

Just to satisfy my curiosity.

Nothing more.

* * *

My interview at GE went as expected: I was offered an entry position in their engineering department where I would be mentored before moving on to real responsibilities. The company set my starting date to coincide with the beginning of their third quarter: July 1.

That left me more than four weeks to find affordable lodging in the city itself or across the river in Brooklyn. Affordable might not be easy since my starting pay was low and I could not share my lodgings—my circumstances dictated that I live alone. Once I solved that problem, I'd move my meager belongings from my Boston rooming house.

But before I did anything, I wanted to visit Nikola Tesla's facility at Wardenclyffe. So I boarded a train that took me seventy miles into the wilds of Long Island, past endless fields of corn and potatoes, past trackless pine forests, to a town called Shoreham. I had intended to ask at the station for directions to Wardenclyffe, but the tower's looming presence dominated the sky as I stepped off. A dirt road ran that way so I followed it; an empty rail siding ran parallel to it.

A short walk brought me to a fenced-in field with a white frame gate like one might see on a cattle ranch. It opened onto a path that led to a red brick building I assumed to be the plant—two stories high with eight tall windows flanking the wide front door. A fanlight capped each of the windows and the door. A brick chimney with a rather ornate spherical damper jutted from the center of the roof, dwarfed by the tower beyond it. On the left toward the rear, an empty freight car sat idle at the end of the rail siding.

Had I known that Tesla kept an office on South Fifth Avenue in the city, I would have made a stop to arrange this visit, but ignorance is bliss, as they say, and by chance I arrived unannounced at a most opportune time.

I stepped through the open front door into a whirlwind of activity, a cacophony of hammering, sawing, shouting, a whining turbine, welding, and even a glassblower at work in a corner. I estimated the square interior at approximately one hundred feet on a side. A second level had been erected along the rear wall, but the front section remained open floor to the ceiling. The same large, fan-light windows along the front also lined the side walls, admitting generous illumination that obviated the need for artificial lighting on such a sunny day as this.

I flagged down a passing workman carrying a long two-by-four. "Is Mister Tesla here?"

"Not sure," he said with a frown, then jerked a thumb toward the rear section. "Go ask George."

"George?"

"George Scherff. He runs the place. He'll know."

I moved across the hot, smoky space to the rear where I spotted a florid-faced man in white shirt sleeves. His dark brown hair was wet with perspiration along his collar as he studied a blueprint.

"Mister Scherff?"

His troubled expression turned to annoyance when he looked at me.

"You cannot be in here," he said. "No reporters."

"I'm not a reporter. I—"

"I don't care who you are, you're trespassing. This is a private facility."

I'd come a long way and was not about to be brushed off.

"I have not traveled from the city simply to satisfy idle curiosity. I have a professional interest."

"'Professional'? What profession?"

"I'm a graduate of MIT with a degree in—"

"MIT?" said an accented voice behind me. "What did you study?"

I turned to face Nikola Tesla himself.

I confess the sight of him struck me dumb for a moment. He was taller than I expected, but no mistaking the dark, center-parted hair, the thick black mustache, and those eyes, those piercing dark eyes. He too was in shirtsleeves, but wore the vest and trousers of a three-piece suit. And spats, of all things. Just a few years shy of fifty, he radiated the energy of a much younger man—a living Tesla coil.

"M-mister Tesla." I confess to making a slight bow. "Charles Atkinson at your service."

Now why did I say *that*?

He smiled. "At my service, is it? Do you plan to put your learning from MIT at my service?"

"No. Yes. I mean…" I was sounding like an idiot.

"What did you study there?"

"Electrical engineering."

His dark eyes lit. "Ah! A kindred spirit. Then you have come to the right place." He extended his hand. "Nikola Tesla, at your service."

We shared a laugh as we shook, but he did not release my hand. Instead he turned it over and looked at my palm.

"Calluses? You have a tanned face and workingman's hands, Mister Atkinson."

Usually people remark on the size of my hands—they're small—not the calluses.

"That is because I *work*, Mister Tesla. My scholarship at MIT did not cover private quarters. I prefer to live alone."

He nodded. "Better for your studies, yes?"

That was not the main reason, but…

"Certainly."

"What kind of work?"

"I work in a warehouse near the Boston docks all the summer when I have no classes and work what hours I can spare during the school year."

He looked me up and down, inventorying my slight frame. I weigh eight and a half stone—about 120 pounds on a US scale.

"You certainly are not what I expect to see when someone tells me they are a warehouseman."

Hard men and hard drinkers doing hard work. As a college boy I could never expect to be accepted by them, and I'd suffered my share of hazing at first—especially because of my size and baby face—but I'd learned never to back down. I could come off like a wolverine, cursing and snarling with the best of them, without striking a blow.

The key was I never shirked my work, and that gradually earned their respect, grudging though it might have been. They were always glad for an extra pair of ready hands, even my small ones. As an added benefit, the work hardened my muscles, while exposure to the elements—I took outside work whenever I could—weathered my baby face. I was happy for both.

He released my hand. "That does not leave much time for a social life."

I forced a grin. "I have *no* social life, sir."

I didn't mention the loneliness—crushing at times. But that was my burden, not his.

He gave me an appraising look. "I was not much older than you when I quit Edison after he cheated me. I dug ditches until I found another job in the electrical field. A man does what he must to keep food in his belly, eh?"

I loved the "man" reference and experienced a sudden kinship that went beyond our interest in electricity.

"You have an accent," he said.

I wanted to tell him that *he* had the accent, just as I'd told all my classmates at MIT when they made fun of the Limey: It's *my* language, I'd say, and *I* know how to speak it. It's merely on loan to you. But I opted for politesse.

"It's British—Mancunian to be specific."

"You came with your family?"

"My parents have passed on to their greater reward."

"Ah, mine too. Then we are both orphans and both immigrants." Another bond. "Tell me your story."

I gave him a heavily edited version, skipping the part that would have me thrown out the door.

"I was born in Manchester in 1878. My father died when I was twelve, my mother when I was nineteen. I sold our cottage and decided

I needed a new life, a fresh start. America beckoned. I landed at Ellis Island, answered the 29 questions, and I was in. I sailed through, I believe, because I spoke English and looked healthy. Even in Manchester I'd heard of MIT. I'd excelled in maths in school and decided to try for it. My score of 90% on their entrance exam guaranteed my acceptance. I now have a degree."

"Excellent. I am an American citizen now," he added with obvious pride.

I nodded. "I intend to become one as soon as possible."

"Good for you. So, what brings you to Wardenclyffe, young man?"

"I spotted the tower from across the Sound and decided I must see firsthand what you are doing."

"No-no," Mr. Scherff said. "We cannot allow that."

Tesla then introduced him as his secretary and accountant and, for the past year or so, the plant manager here at Wardenclyffe.

"Perhaps we can, George."

"But this is just a *boy!*" he said with a sneer.

Though the tone was pejorative, I wasn't offended in the least. But I decided to show my wolverine face.

"Bollocks!" I raised a fist. "Want to step outside and see what this 'boy' can do to your face?"

He laughed but backed up a step. "Now-now. That won't be necessary."

Yes, a dollop of pugnaciousness could carry a long way.

"He has a degree, after all," Tesla said.

Scherff wasn't budging. He snorted. "Talk is cheap."

"Indeed," said Tesla, and then proceeded to quiz me.

He started at a very basic level with Ohm's Law and progressed into more esoteric areas of practical and theoretical electrical concepts. After just a few minutes he smiled and gave a satisfied nod.

"You learned well. I will show you around myself."

"But—" Scherff began.

"I have a good feeling about this young man, George." He turned to me. "You understand that you cannot speak of what I am about to show you."

"Of course."

"Good." He led me back to the littered main floor. "We have

nothing terribly special out here. You can see the glass blower creating our vacuum tubes over there. We have an x-ray machine, a huge stock of wires and cables, as you can imagine. Three resonant transformers—"

"Tesla coils," I said.

"As they are rightly called." He seemed pleased that I'd recognized them. "And here is our coal-fired generator."

"It looks like a Westinghouse."

"It is. Leased from Mister Westinghouse. It supplies two-hundred watts."

"Westinghouse is involved, then?"

"Somewhat." I immediately sensed this was a thorny topic. "J. P. Morgan is our major source of funding."

I spied an odd shape partially covered by a tarp. "Do my eyes deceive me or is that a boat?"

He frowned. "Yes. Last year I closed my Houston Street lab and moved its contents here. That is one of my autonomous craft. It can be controlled from shore or from another craft. I've tried to interest the Navy but they don't see a practical use. Can you imagine?"

A plethora of uses leapt to mind and I said as much.

"See?" he said, slapping me on the back. "You have vision. Would that you were an admiral!" He turned and indicated the enclosed rear section. "Back here we have my office, a kitchen, a library, a laboratory, an instrumentation room with all our controls, a machine shop, a boiler room to supply heat in the winter."

"And what of the tower?" I said. "It fascinates me."

"Oh, it's not just a tower," he said with a sly grin. "What's beneath the tower is just as important. Perhaps more so."

He led me along a passage through the rear section and out the back door. I stopped and gazed up at the tower. It looked positively massive close up. A maze of crisscrossing struts and trusses formed the tapering octagonal base leading up to the circular platform that supported the intricately wired mushroom-cap cupola. A thick steel pipe ran up the center to the top.

"How tall is it?"

"The top of the cupola is exactly one hundred and eighty-seven feet above the ground. For aesthetic reasons we will eventually enclose the base, but the skin has no effect on function." He waved an arm at the structure. "This is what everyone sees, this is what they love to depict in the newspapers. But they don't see the rest of the tower, the part that goes down into the Earth."

"Down?"

"Yes. One hundred-twenty feet. Come."

We walked the hundred feet or so to the tower, then, ducking under trusses, we stepped onto the large concrete base, solid except for the ten-by-twelve-foot opening at its center. Moving closer I could see a shaft plunging into the earth. The pipe running up the center of the tower originated in the shaft. A staircase spiraled down along the steel-lined walls, disappearing into the darkness below. Tesla threw a blade switch on a nearby junction box and a vertical row of bulbs came to life along the length of the shaft.

"Shall we?" he said

"By all means!"

My hand shook as I grasped the rail and followed him down into the Earth. Here was a level of excitement I had not experienced in years—not since my first view of the Statue of Liberty as my ship from Liverpool approached New York Harbor.

Down and around we went along the inner surface of this shaft the height of a medium-size building. The air grew damp and dank, mold and mildew spotted the wood and metal walls. And still we descended.

When we reached the moist floor at the bottom, he said, "We stopped here before we entered the aquifer. This is where most of the money has gone."

I saw four smaller brick-lined passages—wide enough to crawl through—heading off to who-knew-where from the center of each wall.

"What are those?"

"Tunnels running north, south, east, and west. They go back to the surface for ventilation. But this," he said, tapping the central steel pipe, "this runs in the opposite direction. This pushes another three-hundred feet deeper into the Earth."

I think my jaw dropped. We were already twelve stories down.

Now another three hundred feet?

"W-what? Why?"

"To anchor the tower to the Earth. I'm going to make the planet quiver with energy, I'm going to turn the Earth itself into a giant conductor."

He then launched into a frenetic lecture on creating terrestrial standing waves and transmitting power through the Earth itself from one resonance transformer to another. He was mesmerizing.

Here was a man who thought big and placed no boundaries on his imagination—who recognized no limits on what humanity could accomplish if it set its mind to it. A dreamer of fantastic dreams armed with the knowledge and intelligence and audacity to realize those dreams—dreams of worldwide wireless communication and power.

"Energy will be available to everyone," he said. "Like the air we breathe."

I knew at that moment that I had to be part of those dreams. I had to help him make them happen. I wanted my name on the rolls of those who made the dream a reality.

He kept talking theory as we made our way back up to the surface. I barely heard a word. I was seeing the global ramifications of wireless power.

"This will change the whole world!" I said as we reached fresh air again. "Transform civilization! Create a golden age of peace and prosperity!"

He laughed. "I would not be so sure about peace and prosperity—I am certain we'll still find excuses to kill each other. But worldwide wireless will most certainly change the world as we know it."

"Hire me!" I said, shocked that I'd had the audacity to blurt those two words.

He laughed. "I would love to. You have the credentials and you certainly have the enthusiasm. I, however, lack sufficient funds."

"But you said J. P. Morgan—"

"The finances have become very complicated. With your degree I am sure you can secure a good-paying—"

"I already have one. With G.E. I start July the first. But I would gladly give it up to—"

He held up a hand. "Be smart and take that job. Learn all you can there. And perhaps in the future—the near future, I hope—we will have straightened out our finances here and you and I can talk again."

I couldn't give this up—I *wouldn't*.

"I'll be an unpaid intern. It can be my preceptorship, my apprenticeship in wireless energy."

I had savings. I'd used some of the proceeds from the sale of the family cottage to come to America, but my frugal ways and warehouse earnings had allowed me to preserve a small nest egg.

He waved me off. "I could not possibly ask you to—"

"You're not asking *me*—I'm asking *you*."

"Where will you live?"

"Right here! Can we set up a cot on the upper landing? All I'll need is some food."

I could hardly believe I was saying this. I am convinced I'd gone a little barmy then.

He gave me a long look. "You are sure about this?"

I'd never been so bloody sure of anything in my life.

"I can always get a job with an electrical company," I said. "But when will I ever get another chance to change the world?"

He stroked his mustache.

"Do you have a woman?"

The question took me aback. "Why…no."

"You are not involved with a woman, not engaged to be married or anything of that nature?"

"No. Why do you ask?" Not that he had any right to.

"If you are to be apprenticed to me, I must require that you remain celibate during that time. An inventor must not marry. Sir Isaac Newton did not marry, nor did Emmanuel Kant. I do not think you can name many great inventions that have been made by married men."

"I assure you, sir, I have no romantic involvements."

I spoke the truth. Attachment for me was nigh impossible. Though many times, in a fit of longing for companionship, I'd wished otherwise.

"Good. For an artist, a musician, a writer…romance is almost a necessity. But for an inventor, no. Those three must gain inspiration from a woman's influence and be led by their love to finer achievement. But an inventor has so intense a nature, with so much in it of wild, passionate quality, that in giving himself to a woman he might love, he would give everything, and so take everything from his chosen field. Be alone, that is the secret of invention; be alone, that is when ideas are born."

I'd heard Tesla was celibate, but had not expected him to broach the subject with me.

"I repeat, sir, I am unattached."

"Good to hear, and more the pity. For sometimes we feel so lonely."

Oh, how well I knew that.

"George rents a room in Port Jefferson," he went on, "as do I when I visit. I think we might be able to arrange quarters here for you."

"Then I'm hired?"

He laughed and thrust out his hand. "How can I say no to such optimism?"

We shook.

"To changing the world," I cried.

"Yes," he said softly. "To changing the world."

I had no idea that by the time we were through with our work here, that phrase would have taken on a whole new and terrifying meaning.

* * *

My Wardenclyffe apprenticeship did not begin immediately. I had to inform GE that circumstances beyond my control—this sudden obsession with a wireless world certainly seemed beyond my control—would prevent me from accepting the position they offered. No, I would not be joining a competitor and I hoped if circumstances permitted I might return at a future date. I doubted very much that would happen, but I never believed in burning bridges.

Then I had to move all my worldly possessions from Boston to Wardenclyffe. I lived in a furnished apartment so I owned very little. I arrived with suitcases of books and clothing and little else.

The enormity of my decision struck me full force then. I had walked away from a steady-paying job to take an apprenticeship with room and board as my only compensation. I had sacrificed the privacy I so cherished—no, *needed* was a better word—to dwell on the upper level of what was essentially a factory. At least I hadn't had to sacrifice family and friends; I had none of the former and virtually none of the latter. For various reasons I have avoided close relationships since coming to America. I am a solitary man.

Be alone, that is the secret of invention; be alone, that is when ideas are born...

If that proved true, I would evolve into a veritable dynamo of invention.

I strung a wire and used extra sheets to partition the northeast corner of the largely unfinished loft. I slept on a cot under the sloping roof and lived out of my suitcases. We had a latrine outside and fresh water from a well, powered by an electric pump. The local farmers stopped by regularly to sell their eggs and vegetables and occasional cuts of pork or chicken or duck, which I cooked up in the kitchen. At MIT I'd developed a taste for lobsters; when a local fisherman would bring one around now and then, I'd boil it up, crack in open, drench it in local butter, and feast.

Three bicycles had been moved from Tesla's Manhattan lab to Wardenclyffe and I would use one to visit the general store in Shoreham Village for condiments and various sundries. Sunrise shining through the fanlight atop the window in my wall woke me every morning.

Spartan living, to be sure, but I was learning so much at the feet of a genius. Whole new worlds of thought were opening to me.

When Tesla saw my living conditions, he had the carpenters wall off that section of the loft. A door I could bar afforded me the privacy I needed. I settled in for the long haul.

As chief of plant operations, George Scherff was suspicious of me and stand-offish at first, but I quickly won him over with my eagerness to tackle any task he set for me.

As we worked together, he talked, and I learned that the Wardenclyffe finances were teetering on the precipice of ruin. J. P. Morgan had advanced only one third of the $150,000 in funding he'd promised and had refused to transfer the rest.

"If only the maestro would concentrate on wireless communication," Scherff told me, "Morgan might come around. But he insists on combining it with wireless energy which is so much more costly to develop."

"But that's his dream—wireless energy for all."

"Yes, but that is why Morgan is backing off. I heard him tell Tesla, 'If anyone can draw on the power, where do we put the meter?'"

Well, yes, I could see Morgan's point. He hadn't become a captain of industry by giving money away. But didn't he see? Didn't he want a hand in changing the world?

I said, "J. P. Morgan isn't the only fish in the financial sea. There must be others he can interest."

Scherff shook his head. "He has tried. My God, how he has tried. Wined and dined them, sent them gifts, but they are interested only in Marconi."

Perfectly understandable why Marconi's accomplishment, limited though it had been, had sent most investors running his way. Money would gravitate toward the Italian's demonstrated success rather than Tesla's extravagant promises.

"We need a successful demonstration," Scherff told me. "Something spectacular to hold up before the investing world."

Tesla must have felt the same. Before my arrival, he would appear only on weekends, traveling from his rooms at the Waldorf Astoria to arrive with his Serbian manservant and a huge basket of food. Now he was here every day, sans Serb.

By mid-July we were ready for a test. Not an actual transmission—we were nowhere near ready for that yet—but a test of the components, their connections, and the generator to see if we could get them all working together. We had a Tesla coil installed in the bottom of the shaft and another in the cupola of the tower.

We waited until well after sundown when it was full dark. All the workers had been sent home, leaving just the three of us to man the equipment. By that time, we had little left to do. I shoveled extra coal into the generator to keep it at maximum—hot work in July, though my only concession to the heat was to roll up my sleeves. Its output could reach 200 watts but the Tesla coils could multiply that to one million or more.

At about 10 P.M., when all was ready, George Scherff and I stood by the back door and waited for Tesla—he deserved the honor—to throw the switch inside.

Fog often rolled off the Sound after dark, but not tonight. The Milky Way smeared across a cloudless sky. In my solitary life I assuaged my loneliness at night by identifying the planets and constellations. At another time of year I might have looked for Orion but I knew it rose at dawn during the summer. So I contented myself with finding the Big Dipper; I followed a line from the leading edge of its cup to Polaris, the North Star, twinkling above the tower's cupola.

We heard a deep hum and knew he'd thrown the switch. By the time Tesla joined us, the sparks had begun to fly, growing larger and longer and brighter as the coils above and below multiplied and magnified the voltage. I stood mesmerized by the magnificent electrical display. No July Fourth fireworks could compete with this. And lest you think I exaggerate, here was what the misspelling-prone *New York Sun* had to say the following day:

TESLA'S FLASHES STARTLING
But He Won't Tell Us What He Is
Trying For At Wardencliffe

Wardencliffe, L. I., July 16—Natives hereabouts are intensely interested in the electrical display shown from the tall tower and poles in the grounds where Nicola Tesla is conducting his experiments in wireless telegraphy and telephony. All sorts of lightning were flashed from the tall tower and poles last night. For a time the air was filled with blinding streaks of electricity which seemed to shoot off into the darkness on some mysterious errand. The display continued until after midnight.

Perhaps he was correct about it lasting past midnight, perhaps not. I was not watching the clock. We were too busy taking readings, measuring voltages, and checking connections.

I do recall a strange feeling in my chest. I didn't know how to explain it other than a sense of something *wrong*. I tried to pin it down but could not. Everything in my life at the moment was as right as could be, so why should I feel this sudden unease?

And another thing: I remember looking up at the stars at one point and seeing no trace of the Milky Way. Nor did I recognize any of the constellations. I didn't pay this any mind at the time, blaming it on interference from the high-voltage flashes. But this would take on dreadful significance in the time to come.

* * *

We were all in high spirits the next morning, laborers included. Almost all were local and they'd witnessed the display from their homes; it had convinced them they were involved in a project of major significance.

A man named James Warden, however, wore a concerned expression when he showed up midmorning. I had not seen him before but Tesla and Scherff seemed to know him well.

"Quite a display you put on last night," he said after greetings and handshakes.

"Just an equipment test," Tesla said.

"What were you transmitting?"

"Nothing. As I said, just testing connections and such."

He stared at Tesla a moment, then said, "Come down to the waterline with me. I want to show you something."

"Is there a problem?" Tesla said.

"Yes, I believe there is."

"Are you going to tell us what?" Scherff said.

"I think it best you see for yourselves."

"We were nowhere near the water."

Warden nodded. "Perhaps, but I do think you should see this."

We walked out the back into the thick fog bank that had rolled off the Sound; the tower appeared oddly truncated as its cupola had been swallowed by the mist. Warden led the way with Tesla beside him. I followed with Scherff.

"Do I assume he's the 'Warden' in Wardenclyffe?" I said.

"He's a land developer who owns most of Shoreham." He waved an arm around. "From the train station down to the Sound. He made the maestro a good deal on these two hundred acres, but not from the goodness of his heart. He has plans to build houses and sell them to all the employees once we're up and running."

Once we're up and running...

That might take a while. Last night's run had proved that all the components were functioning, but we had sent no messages.

Tesla had purchased the acreage closest to the rail line, so the walk to the Sound was nearly a mile through the remnants of a huge potato farm. An eerie walk in a misty limbo. The two ahead appeared to be in deep conversation.

"What are they discussing so seriously?" I said.

Scherff hesitated, then, "Money, of course."

"How can you be so sure?"

"Because I pay all the bills—or do not pay them."

I got the impression from his tone that unpaid bills outnumbered those he paid.

"I don't understand."

"It is not your concern."

I took the hint and changed the subject.

"This Warden chap is being rather mysterious. I wonder what he wants us to see."

Scherff only shrugged.

As the end of our walk neared, the keening cries and squawks of sea birds filled the air. Soon the fog-streaked Long Island Sound came into view. Flapping seagulls and terns crowded the shore. They rose in a cloud at our approach. Warden stopped about a dozen feet short of the waterline and pointed.

"There. Are you responsible for that?"

At first I didn't know what he meant, and then I realized the sandy shore was littered with hundreds and hundreds of dead fish. That explained the birds. We'd interrupted their breakfast buffet.

"Bloody hell," I said, moving closer. "What could have done this?"

"I've lived along the North Shore most of my life," Warden said, "and I've never seen a fish kill like this. It has to be related to your

32

fireworks display last night."

"I cannot imagine the connection," Tesla said.

Scherff came up beside me. "Wait a minute. Something is wrong here."

"I'm very well aware of that," Warden said. "Something killed these fish."

"No," Scherff said. "These fish killed themselves."

We all turned to stare at him. Finally Warden said, "That's preposterous!"

"Wait-wait." Scherff gave a soft laugh. "Don't look at me like I'm crazy. I'm not saying they were suicidal. I'm simply saying they jumped out of the water."

Warden harrumphed—yes, a genuine *harrumph*. "How can you possibly know that?"

I wanted an answer myself.

Scherff stepped over the dead fish and moved closer to the water where he pointed to a wavering line of seaweed.

"All right, look here. This is obviously the high-water mark."

No question. The sand on the Sound side was flat and smooth. The sand on the land side was anything but. The dead fish lay a number of feet beyond the high-tide line.

Scherff pointed back and forth between the tide line and the fish. "How did they get from here to there? Obviously they jumped." He frowned. "And that bothers me. That bothers me very much."

"Why?" Tesla said. "Fish jump. I have seen them."

"Not all fish jump. And look at the variety of these fish. It's not as if some school lost its way. I see shad, weakfish, scup, and puffers along with sea robins and fluke."

"I fail to see the significance," Warden said.

Scherff sent him a penetrating look. "You say you've lived out here all your life. I haven't, but I love to fish the Sound. I go on group boats out of Oyster Bay whenever I can."

"I know Oyster Bay well," Warden said.

Didn't everyone? President Roosevelt had a home there.

"The point is," Scherff said, "I know my fish. What do you know of sea robins and fluke?"

33

Warden shrugged. "Not much except the first is inedible and the second is delicious."

"But do you know where they live?"

"Of course. They're bottom fish."

"Exactly! They live on the bottom." He nudged a particularly ugly fish with the toe of his shoe. "They call this a sea robin but it can't fly. It's a slow, clumsy fish and, as you say, not for eating, so not worth catching. How did it go from the bottom of the water to end here on the sand? Likewise with the fluke. A much faster fish but still, not a leaping fish."

"Maybe they were attracted to all your flashing lights last night," Warden said.

I saw Tesla's face darken. "Then you would see this after every violent thunderstorm. No, something else is at work here."

Warden stubbornly shook his head. "You put on your show and the fish die. The connection is obvious."

He was offering a perfect example of a common logical fallacy. *Post hoc, ergo propter hoc*: If B follows A, then A must have caused B. But I did not feel it my place to speak up.

Many of the bigger fish appeared wounded, seemed to have suffered deep, linear, finger-width cuts along their flanks. If I didn't think it impossible, I might have characterized them as burns. I was about to mention this when we were interrupted.

A barefooted elderly woman had appeared out of the fog from the east, an aging golden retriever ambling at her side. She wore a patterned blouse and a mismatched ankle-length skirt; she'd wrapped her gray hair in a plaid scarf. She had swarthy skin and a hook nose. Gold hoops swung from her earlobes. What was a Gypsy woman doing out here?

She stopped within a few feet of us and pointed to the dead fish.

"This should not be," she said in a thick accent I couldn't quite identify. "Is not a good thing."

"Yes," Warden said testily. "We are quite well aware of that. Do you have anything else to contribute?"

"I have much to contribute, especially to this man."

She stepped up to Tesla and jabbed a finger toward his startled face as she spoke in a foreign tongue.

"Who are you?" Warden said when she'd finished. "And where did you come from?"

"Everywhere," she said and walked on, her dog beside her. "From everywhere I come."

Tesla, his expression troubled, watched her go.

"What did she say?" I asked.

He shook his head. "Nothing."

I very much doubted that.

"What language was that?"

"Serbian."

As she walked off into the fog, she called back without turning her head.

"You are thinking fish leaping *toward* something? Look again. See how far they jump—even bottom dwellers. No, were running *from* something." As she disappeared her final disembodied words echoed from the mist. "Something scare fish—scare so much are leaping onto dry land to escape."

* * *

Leaving James Warden by the Sound, we headed back to the plant, discussing the mysterious fish kill along the way. However that was forgotten when we reached the plant and Tesla saw the latest edition of the *Sun*. The story about the tower's electrical display prompted a decision.

"We must confine all further testing to the daylight hours. I don't want everything that goes wrong along the North Shore blamed on our experiments."

"The flashes will still be visible," Scherff said.

"But much less noticeable, and not at such a great distance. We will take advantage of the fogs whenever we can."

"Well, today is as foggy as we'll ever see," I said. "Shall we give it another go?"

Tesla gazed at one of the high, south-facing windows where the fog seemed to press against the glass, then nodded. "We shall."

And we did. Same procedure as the night before. We knew all the connections were good, but would they hold up under the electrical load Tesla wanted to put through them?

He didn't send the workers home. I think he wanted to see how aware they would be of the testing. Their only involvement was indirect: He kept them continually stoking the coal fire of the generator.

Fog still shrouded the cupola when he threw the switch. We heard the hum of the coils and the crackle of the bolts, saw their muted flashes through the mist, but the workers remained unaware due to the noise level within the building.

But once again, standing outside between the rear door and the tower, I had that same uncomfortable sensation, that *wrongness* deep in my chest. I pressed a hand over my sternum and turned to Tesla and Scherff, standing nearby.

"Do you feel anything…in here?"

Scherff shook his head. "No."

"Like what?" Tesla said.

"I-I'm not sure." I felt somewhat foolish. "Almost like…fear."

Both cast me dubious looks.

Tesla said, "It is most likely the electromagnetic field created by the tower. You are simply sensitive to it."

I knew quite a bit about electromagnetism, and had indeed experimented with its effects in my studies. This was quite different. I was sure that even if I enclosed myself within a Faraday cage I would feel this. I was similar to Tesla and Scherff in so many ways, yet knew we were also fundamentally different, a difference that might explain why I sensed what they couldn't.

But that subject was off limits, so I let the matter drop.

After an hour we shut off the power and the wrongness receded. Relieved, I joined them in checking the connections for signs of overload damage.

We found none, so Tesla decided on a twenty-five percent increase next test.

That opportunity presented itself two days later during another pea-soup fog. And once again I experienced that *wrong* feeling, only this time it seemed more intense. Proportional to the power Tesla was feeding the tower? As before, Tesla and Scherff remained oblivious.

Upon subsequent inspection, the increased power had caused no damage to the circuits.

That afternoon, the three of us gathered in the quiet chaos of Tesla's office. The desk and all his files from the Hudson Street lab had wound up here—or perhaps I should say had been dumped here. He sat in a chair behind a desk piled high with paper. Scherff and I seated ourselves on boxes.

"With these three test runs," Tesla said, "we have been sending energy into the atmosphere and through the Earth in a diffuse and unmonitored manner, without an attempt to document the range. Now that we know the circuitry is sound, we can test the range of energy transmission. We must decide now how best to do that."

"Why not use the same method as Colorado Springs?" Scherff said.

I was only vaguely familiar with that. "Was that when you lit fifty-watt bulbs miles from the transmitter?"

Tesla nodded. "Two-point-six miles, to be precise."

The distance startled me. "Why doesn't the world know this?"

"Because the world is not ready to believe, and less than three miles, in the grand scheme of things, is nothing."

I couldn't argue that.

"But if things were going that well, why did you leave Colorado?"

Tesla glanced at Scherff, then said, "Money, as usual. I ran out of it."

"One hundred thousand dollars consumed in eight months."

"But worth it!" Tesla said, pounding his desk. "I learned much and filed new patents." He spread his arms. "But everything comes to fruition here."

Exactly what I wanted to hear—exactly *why* I was here.

"Tell me what you need me to do and consider it done."

"That's the spirit!" he said and we started making our plans.

As the meeting broke up, with the promise that we would concretize our tentative plans over the weekend, I waited for George to leave, then approached Tesla.

"Can you tell me now what the Gypsy woman said to you?"

He frowned, hesitated, then shook his head. "It was nonsense. Not worth repeating."

"But—"

"Not worth repeating," he said in a firmer tone.

I backed off the subject. If he said it was nonsense, then it probably was. As for me, I was too filled with the excitement of endless possibilities stretching before us to worry about it.

At least until the next morning when I saw a newspaper belonging to one of the workers.

* * *

Tesla and Scherff had yet to arrive from their Port Jefferson lodgings. I'd fried some eggs and potatoes and settled down to peruse a borrowed paper as I ate. I stopped in mid chew when I read that a barn had disappeared yesterday in Rocky Point, the hamlet just to the west of Wardenclyffe.

A small barn, according to the article, but size was irrelevant: How could an entire building simply disappear? An eye witness—a Mrs. Williams, owner of the property with her husband—claimed to have watched the building "flaking off" and disappearing into the fog, along with the horse they had quartered there.

Normally I would have laughed it off, but the mention of the fog caught my attention. I'd skimmed the article. This time I read it more carefully and noticed that the witness's statement included the time of the occurrence...the barn had disappeared yesterday during the hour of our third test of the tower.

Coincidence, I was sure. And yet...that feeling I had whenever the tower was powered...that feeling that something was not right...

Two pages later I came upon another short piece about the release from the hospital of a Sound Beach groundskeeper named Timothy Herring after treatment for burns he'd suffered while cleaning a swimming pool.

Burns? From a swimming pool?

The incident reportedly happened on Tuesday, the day of our

second test. Sound Beach was another nearby hamlet, just west of Rocky Point.

Hadn't some of the dead fish I'd seen appeared burned?

I lost my appetite. I'd always been a practical sort, never one to let my imagination run wild, but my odd feelings and these even odder incidents had kindled a fire of worrisome possibilities. Questions assaulted me and I was determined to see them answered.

The train with Tesla and Scherff wasn't due for another 40 minutes but I couldn't wait. I grabbed one of the bicycles and travelled west along the county road that paralleled the tracks. I had no idea where I was going, no idea where Shoreham and Wardenclyffe ended and Rocky Point began. I saw no signs, but I knew I was looking for a farm. The thick pine woods to my left precluded agriculture of any sort, so I focused my attention to the right. It couldn't be far. The hamlets out here were small—maybe two miles on a side at most—and the farm properties relatively large.

Somehow I passed through Rocky Point without seeing the farm. I did however come upon a large estate in Sound Beach bordered by a dry stone wall with a cozy gatehouse guarding the entrance.

I knocked on the gatehouse door with the intent of asking directions to the Williams farm, but when I saw the bandaged arms and neck of the stubby man who answered, I realized I had serendipity working for me.

After a quick glance at the newspaper I'd brought along, I said, "You wouldn't happen to be Timothy Herring, would you?"

"I would." He jutted his chin at the newspaper in the bike's basket. "And I suppose you been reading about me."

"I have, sir. I read about your burns and I wonder if you might relate the circumstances to me."

He could have been fifty or seventy years of age, badly in need of a shave, wearing bib overalls over a short-sleeve shirt. He eyed me suspiciously.

"You another of them reporters?"

"I assure you, I am not. I'm staying not far away and I'm curious as to the time of day you suffered these burns. On Tuesday, am I correct?"

He nodded. "Tuesday midday. Up at the pool. I always skim the pool midday."

Tuesday midday…the exact time of our second test. My unease grew.

"Where's the pool?"

"Behind the house."

"Fancy a stroll up there?" I needed to see this.

"You talk funny, young fella."

"I'm British. We all talk funny. Shall we go?"

He hesitated, obviously not anxious to return to the site of his injuries, but also not wanting to show fear. Finally he decided on the manly thing to do.

"Follow me."

He led me up a rising stone driveway past a granite mansion.

"What exactly happened?" I said.

"Wait'll we get there and I'll show you."

He rambled on about other matters, how he could use help maintaining the grounds, how he hadn't been back to the pool since Tuesday, and how the Ainsleys—the owners—came out from their Fifth Avenue townhouse on weekends in the summer and would be arriving early afternoon.

As we crossed the rear of the estate we were rewarded with a beautiful view of the Long Island Sound. The tower loomed over the trees to the east, but I decided it best not to mention any connection to Wardenclyffe.

He waved at the Sound. "Why you need a pool when you got all that out there is beyond me, but that ain't none of my business."

He stopped about a hundred feet from the pool where a long-handled net lay on the grass.

"Do me a favor," he said, handing me the net pole. He looked unsettled, perhaps even frightened. "Take this and go have a look at the bottom, will ya?"

His attitude made me uneasy, and so now came my turn to hide any show of fear. I walked the rest of the way with all the nonchalance I could muster. Slate tiles surrounded the pool, as did tables, chairs, and furled umbrellas. A steady breeze flowed off the Sound. The pool itself was lined with white tiles and rested within a concrete coping.

I don't know what I expected to see when I reached the edge but, except for dead leaves floating on the surface of slightly cloudy water, it appeared quite empty. Why did he want me to have a look at the bottom?

I called back, "What about the bottom?"

"Can you see the tiles at the deep end?"

An odd question. "Yes."

"Take the net and touch it to the bottom there."

Curiouser and curiouser, but I did as he asked. The net pole ran perhaps ten feet in length but the pool's deep end was barely six. I bounced the net against the bottom tiles.

"I'm doing that."

Herring came up beside me and took the pole. After a few test touches against the bottom, he said, "Wasn't like this on Tuesday."

"What was different?"

"The bottom at the deep end was black…blackest black I ever seen. The water itself was clear, mind you. Just the bottom was black. Like it had been painted or the like. We had us a fog that day, if you remember."

"I do." I did indeed.

"Well, I thought the black might have something to do with that. A trick of the light, you see, although I never seen nothing like it before. Anyways, I stuck the pole into the water to scrape the net along the bottom and see if the black would come loose, in case it was some sorta dirt. Well, the net keeps going down, don't you know."

"I don't understand," I said. "You mean you dropped it?"

"No, I didn't drop it." His tone became annoyed. "I been doing this every day every summer for more years'n you been alive. I'm saying the pool is six foot deep at this end and the pole is ten feet long and it kept going straight down six, seven, eight, nine feet into the black—all the way except for the handle in my hand."

He had to be mistaken. "How…how is that possible?"

"It ain't possible, young fella. Ain't possible at all. And what's more, I couldn't see the net. Like the blackness down there had swallowed the end of the pole. I kept pulling it back and shoving it down again and again, trying to reach bottom but not touching nothing. I was about to give up and look for a longer pole when I hit something."

"The bottom."

"No…not the bottom." He'd been talking at a normal volume, but now his voice lowered to just above a whisper. "Not hard like tile. Firm, yeah, but softer." He clinked the net against the bottom. "Hear that? That's tile. This made no sound. I pushed again, harder, and then harder still. *Something* was down there. But what, I couldn't imagine."

He fell silent, staring into the water. I wanted to ask him about the burns but sensed he was getting to that.

"And then?"

"And then…" He took a deep breath. "And then the pole was pulled from my grip. No, not 'pulled,' *snatched*—snatched right from my hands to disappear below. I mean to tell you, it was gone. No sign of it."

"But it was here on the lawn when we came up," I said.

"I know damn well where it was when we came up, but it was pulled from my hands to disappear into the black, and then a few seconds later it come flying out of the water to sail over my head and land behind me."

"How is that—?"

"Wait," he said, holding up a finger. "Wait. I ain't through. As I turned to go get the pole, my ankle suddenly felt like it had been set on fire." He pointed to his left ankle. "I looked down to see a long black rope—at least at first sight I thought it a rope. It was trailing out of the pool and wrapped around my ankle."

"Bloody hell!"

"Bloody hell is right! That wasn't no rope. It was alive and it was pulling me toward the water."

I swallowed. "You're having me on."

He turned on me, shaking his fist in my face. "I am not! The police thought I'd been nipping at the bottle, especially when they looked in the pool and found nothing but empty water. But they weren't here when that rope, that *tendril* wrapped around me."

It seemed best not to challenge him further, so I went along. "Was it like an octopus tentacle—you know, with suckers and the like?"

"No, it was smooth and round like a rope. And *strong.* I tell you, I did a tour out West with the Nineteenth Infantry during the Cheyenne Wars, and I thought I'd never again be as scared as I was doing hand-to-hand combat with those savages. But I tell you true, young fella, and I ain't ashamed to say it: I pissed myself."

"Oh," I said, at a loss as to how to respond.

For a man like this to admit such a level of fear...

"It pulled me off my feet and dragged me along these slates here. I was able to stop my slide by wedging my boots against the coping, but only for a little bit, because another tendril come out and looped around this arm." He held up his right. "It knew exactly where to go—like it could see! A third wrapped around my left leg and I was lost. I screamed like a damsel in distress as I was dragged over the coping and into the water."

"Dear God!"

"God was nowhere in sight, young fella. I was pulled down through the water and into the blackness and I was sure I'd drawn my last breath when suddenly the water started churning. I was spun around and found myself facing the tiles at the bottom of the pool. I made it back to the surface and pulled myself onto land. As I got my wind back, I calmed down, but that was when I noticed the pain. My arm and both legs—ain't never felt such pain."

"How did you get to the police?"

"I dragged myself to the house and used the phone there. They thought I was drunk or crazy. Same with the doctors. Thought I'd imagined the whole thing. But you tell me." He pulled back the bandage on his left forearm. "You tell me if I imagined that!"

I saw a deep linear burn layered with a dark ointment. It resembled the burns I'd seen on the larger fish along the shoreline Tuesday morning.

"Doctors said they look like acid burns. What they didn't say is that they think I burned myself. But we ain't got no acid 'round here, so how did I do it? And *why* would I burn myself? Answer me that?"

He seemed close to tears at the injustice of it all.

"I...I don't believe you did any such thing," I said, and meant it. "But why do you think it released you?"

He smoothed the bandage back into place. "Who can say? I'm more interested in what 'it' was and how 'it' got into the pool and how a six-foot pool got a lot deeper and darker, but most of all I want to know if 'it' is ever coming back. There's a damn good chance I'm going to lose my job when the Ainsleys hear about this, but you know what? If there's a chance that thing might come back, I don't care."

"Certainly understandable," I said.

He turned east and pointed to the tower. "You think that thing could be the cause?"

I feigned ignorance. "I've seen it, of course—who out here hasn't?—But I don't know what it's for."

"That Tesla fellow. Supposedly gonna give free electricity to everyone. Don't know about that, but I do know I seen flashes through the fog when I come up here to clean the pool, and they'd stopped by the time I crawled out of the water all burnt and half drownded. So maybe…"

I waited, silently pleading that he would not blame the tower for his misfortune.

Finally he shrugged. "Ah, who knows? And who'd believe it anyway. Now, if you'll excuse me, I've wasted enough time here. I got work to do."

Relieved, I watched as he stalked off toward the mansion. I called after him: "Before you go, can I ask just a few more questions?"

"No!" was all he said without slowing his pace.

Then I remembered my other mission.

"Well then, can you at least tell me how I might find the Williams farm?"

"Head east," he said without looking back. "Look for the big rock on the north side of the road."

As I made my way back to the gatehouse and my bicycle, I tried to sort out what Timothy Herring had told me. Was he a secret opium smoker who had dreamed the whole thing? Certainly it had all the aspects of a fantastic nightmare.

But the burns…how to explain the burns?

Something bothered me even more, however: the timing of his story. The incident coincided with our Tuesday test of the tower—his spotting the flashes through the fog confirmed it. Had the standing waves we generated in the Earth caused him to hallucinate? Had the wireless power we released caused the burns? After all, the tower stood less than five miles away.

As I pedaled along the county road I concluded that certain people might be sensitive to the tower's emanations, and that these people might react in strange ways—hallucinations, for instance.

It seemed possible—at least not impossible—and I took comfort in the hypothesis.

Riding back along the road, I spotted the rock Herring had mentioned within the first mile or so. It marked the start of a rutted drive a few hundred yards in length, ending at a tidy house with white-washed walls and a cedar shake roof. As I pedaled up the drive, I was once again aware of the tower looming to my right, larger now that I was closer.

A man answered my knock and said his wife was not available to any more reporters and asked if I was another one. My fervent denials must have convinced him, for when I asked to see the barn, he said, "There is no barn, but I'll show you where it was."

He led me across the grassy field west of the house. The entire rear acreage, down to the Sound, was planted with waist-high corn.

"Is Mrs. Williams well?" I said.

"What do you mean by that?" he said, his tone suddenly testy. "Are you asking if she's sound of mind?"

"No-no. Not at all. I—"

"That's what others are saying, but I assure you, you will never find a woman with her feet more firmly on the ground than my wife."

"Please understand that I'm just saying that the incident, as described in this morning's paper, must have been very upsetting."

I didn't mention my doubts. A house "flaking off" and disappearing…how was such a thing possible? And then again, how was such a thing as Mr. Herring described possible?

"Extremely upsetting. We lost our horse. She was very attached to Annabelle."

We stopped before a rectangular patch of bare earth.

"Well, there you have it."

"This is it?" I said, staring. "Is there nothing left?"

He shook his head. "Not a thing. Even the concrete footings are gone."

"When…when did this happen?"

"About midday, I'd say. The barn was whole and fine when I went into the fields in the morning, but when I returned for lunch I found my wife kneeling here on the grass, hysterical. And the barn was gone."

"How is that possible?" I said.

"It's the tower," said a female voice behind me.

I turned to see a haggard-looking woman in a worn, faded house-dress.

"Amelia," said the man. "I don't think—"

"I'm all right, Fred. I can't sit in that house all day."

"The tower?" I said, hoping I might come up with a way to turn her from that thought. "How could it possibly—?"

"The flashes started around noon—I could see them through the fog as I came out with a bucket of fresh water for Annabelle. That was when the barn started trembling."

Trembling?

"I don't understand."

"Have you ever seen a frightened dog during a thunderstorm?"

I nodded. *Vibrating* was perhaps a better word but I didn't suggest it.

"Well, that was what the barn started doing—trembling like it was afraid. I was inside it so I rushed out because I thought we might be having an earthquake. I've read about them though we've never had one in these parts. But the ground outside was still. That didn't stop the barn from trembling, though. And then it started flaking."

"I read that in the paper," I said. "Could you explain?"

"It started on the west wall. Just the paint at first, chipping off in little paper-thin squares, like confetti, and fluttering through the air and into the fog. But it didn't stop with the paint. The wood siding started flaking and flying off and soon the whole west wall was gone. I could see Annabelle in her stall, facing the other way as she drank from her bucket. She didn't seem the least bit disturbed. I shouted to her to get out of there but she kept on drinking. Even when her hindquarters started flaking away, she didn't seem to notice. I kept screaming to her but she didn't seem to hear me."

"Her…her hindquarters?"

I tried to picture it but failed.

"Yes! Little bits of flesh and little drops of blood streaming away. And when they were gone, you'd expect her to fall, wouldn't you? I mean, a four-legged animal without its hind legs will fall, won't it? But she didn't. She just stood there as the flaking slowly ate her away. And soon she was *gone!*"

This last word was propelled by a sob.

My mouth worked soundlessly. I had no idea what to say. The woman's grief was genuine—palpable. I finally resorted to platitudes.

"I'm so sorry, Mrs. Williams. It must have been awful."

"Awful?" she said, her voice rising. "It was horrible beyond words. And it didn't stop with Annabelle. The flaking kept going, eating the side walls and the roof and the hay and the flooring and finally the east wall until nothing was left. I thought our house would be next, but the house was never touched. Just the barn. And that was when I noticed that the flashes from the tower had stopped."

My tongue was sand. Could this have actually happened? It seemed insane. The skeptical scientific corner of my mind began asking if these people were barmy. Had there ever been a barn and an Annabelle?

But Amelia's genuine terror and grief overrode all that.

Something had happened here and, if this woman was to be believed, the events had coincided with our last test of the tower.

Correlation does not equal cause and effect…I kept repeating that.

"It's the tower," she said.

Her tone had a note of finality, but I hazarded a question. "Are you sure the flashes came from the tower?"

"Everyone saw the display Monday night. They came from the same place."

I sensed an opening here. "I saw that too. Quite impressive. Did you observe any strange occurrences here Monday night or the next morning?"

"Well, no," she said, her conviction wavering just a bit.

"I saw a lot of flashes in the fog on Tuesday, as well. Did anything around here flake off then?"

"Hey, whose side are you on?" her husband said.

"I'm simply collecting data," I said. "I just spoke to a grounds man in Sound Beach who received mysterious burns on Tuesday."

Mr. Williams nodded. "Yeah, I read about that. Have you come up with anything?"

"Too soon to say. I'm looking for a consistent pattern and so far I haven't found one. But I'll make the results public as soon as I have something to report."

With that half-truth hanging in the air, I made hasty excuses and left them standing at the site of their vanished barn.

All the way back to Wardenclyffe I reviewed the facts as I knew them. I had circumstantial evidence that the fish—malodorous, bird-pecked, and fly-blown—had leaped from the Sound a good many hours before I saw them, very possibly during the tower's hours of activation the night before. Even so, the fish kill and the groundkeeper's burns were, in and of themselves, relatively minor incidents. But an entire barn disappearing into the fog…that escalated the incidents beyond bizarre into the fantastic—and coincided with the twenty-five percent increase in the power feed to the tower.

Was there a link? My brain rebelled at the possibility, but my gut said *yes*.

What I thought and felt were of little consequence, however. As a mere apprentice I had no authority at Wardenclyffe. All decisions flowed from Tesla. But I'd certainly lay out my findings for him. I was anxious to hear what he had to say on the matter.

* * *

All thoughts of strange phenomena vanished like the morning fog when I returned to Wardenclyffe. A strange freight car sat on the siding. Inside the plant I found a crew of strangers disassembling the generator.

Our own work crews stood silent, watching. I spotted George Scherff pacing outside Tesla's closed office door, arms folded across his chest, and ran up to him.

"What's this all about?"

His quick glance my way revealed a world of pain. "They are re-possessing the generator."

"Who?"

"The Westinghouse people."

"Here now, they can't do that!" I cried.

"I am afraid it is too late for that." He waved a fistful of papers in the air. "Non-payment and breach of contract."

"We've got to get this sorted! I have some money. I can—"

"*Many* missed payments, young Charles. Many, many. You do not have enough."

"But without a generator we…we…"

"Correct. We cannot do anything. All experimentation comes to a halt."

Hands on hips, I began walking in circles. How? Why? First the strange data I'd collected this morning, and now this. My head was ready to explode.

I kicked an empty box. "No generator! He might as well shut down the building!"

"That might be done for him." His expression bleak, Scherff pulled some sheets from the sheaf in his hand. "This was delivered this morning."

I took it and gave it the quickest of reads. I needed no more.

"James Warden is suing him?"

"For non-payment of taxes on the property."

"How can this be, George?" My anger needed a target and Scherff was handy. "Aren't you his accountant? Aren't you supposed to be paying the bills?"

He didn't bother looking at me. "One cannot draw water from a dry well."

He had to be as angry and disappointed as I—more so, since he'd been with Tesla so much longer. But he showed nothing. I wished he'd put aside his bloody Teutonic stoicism and shout or stamp his feet or break something. But that wasn't Scherff's way.

"He is a brilliant man," he added. "Certainly the most brilliant mind of his generation, and perhaps the most brilliant mind in human history. But he has no sense of how to do business. I try to help, but he goes his own way. He should be a billionaire now."

"Billionaire?" I said, astonished. "With a 'B'? How so?"

"His original deal with Westinghouse in exchange for all his AC patents included a royalty of two-and-a-half dollars per horsepower of electricity sold."

"Per horsepower?" My mind was having difficulty grasping this. "Why...by now that must total..."

"Billions. Just as I said."

"But then why...?"

"Do you know anything of 'the current war'?"

"I'm familiar with it."

I knew that during the closing decade of the last century, Edison and Westinghouse had battled in the press and in public over which method of delivering electricity to the country—via direct or alternating current—would prevail. Edison's people went about electrocuting animals small and large—even an elephant at one point— and finally a prisoner on Sing Sing's death row to demonstrate the "danger" of AC. Ultimately they failed. AC was adopted everywhere because of its inherent superiority and practicality.

"What you probably don't know is that it nearly ruined Westinghouse. A Pyrrhic victory in every sense. His AC power was going to light the continent, but he was in danger of losing the company. So in 1896 George Westinghouse came to Tesla and asked him to renegotiate the royalty."

"And Tesla...?" My lips refused to form the fatal word.

Scherff nodded. "Agreed. Yes."

I was speechless for a moment. Finally I said..."Why?"

"Because Westinghouse had always treated him fairly. The maestro values that. He saw a trusted associate in dire straits and knew only one way to respond: He renegotiated a drastically reduced royalty to help the company regain its financial footing."

"He didn't have to make the reduction permanent! He could have made it temporary!"

Scherff's smile was deeply bitter. "Ah, you have a head for business, I see. Yes, that is exactly what I would have advised him, but we would not meet until the following year, and by then it was too late." One of his Germanic shrugs. "Though I doubt he would have listened to me anyway."

"But…but…if he had made it temporary he would quite literally be swimming in money now. He would never have to ask anyone to invest in him again. Not a dime!"

I wasn't sure what to think of Tesla then. A fool, a naïf, or a sublimely decent human being. I hadn't known him long enough to tell.

"Where is he?" I said.

"In his office."

"*How* is he?"

"Not well."

I stepped behind him and knocked on Tesla's door. I waited in vain for his customary "Come." I entered anyway.

Tesla sat behind his desk, his head bowed and clasped between his palms.

"Sir, there must be something we can do."

He did not speak, did not move.

"Sir, just tell me what to do and I'll do it."

Still he did not speak or look up, but moved one of his hands to wave me off. I was dismissed. I left him and returned to Scherff's side.

"You were right," I said. "He's not well."

I was worried about him. He seemed to be heading for a nervous breakdown.

"There must be a way to turn this around," I said.

"I am open to suggestions."

"He's the world's most famous inventor. There must be investors out there he can tap for funds."

"If this were last year, you would be right. But ever since January, it's Marconi-Marconi-Marconi."

He was referring to President Roosevelt's transatlantic message from Massachusetts to King Edward in my homeland using Marconi's apparatus. Word of that spread across the globe like wildfire. A new age of communication was dawning and Marconi was its sun—using Tesla's patents.

"But he still has *some* royalty income from his inventions," I said. "If we all tighten our belts—"

"How?"

"Well, is it necessary for him to live at the Waldorf Astoria?"

A laugh—genuine laugh from George Scherff. "How will that help when he does not pay his hotel bills anyway? Not once since he moved in has he paid his Waldorf bills! He owes the hotel more than fifteen thousand dollars!"

The staggering sum left me speechless. He owed Westinghouse, Suffolk County, the Waldorf Astoria—I was afraid to ask who else.

"It's just as well we're losing the generator," he added.

"How can you say that?"

He waved the sheaf again. "Because we have just received notice that our coal supplier is cutting us off for non-payment. But in the matter of royalties, there's more to the story."

His ominous tone made me want to cover my ears, but I needed to know.

"Go ahead."

"His AC patents run out in two years, so even those reduced royalties will stop in 1905."

Disaster followed by catastrophe. Could this get any worse?

Feeling weak, I stepped away and seated myself on an empty crate.

"Then I guess the dream is over."

I'd spurned the job at GE to help a genius change the world, and now here I sat, not two months later, with nothing but dashed hopes to show for my efforts. I felt like fairytale Jack, trading the family cow for a handful of beans I'd been convinced were magical.

"Do not give up yet," Scherff said. "The maestro always finds a way. And when he cannot, a way finds him."

Not this time, I thought. He's too deep in debt.

Feeling lower than I could ever recall in my life, I slunk up to my quarters and lay down on the cot. Here was when I felt my isolation the most. I longed for a companion, someone to share my heartbreak, offer a shoulder to cry on. But I lay alone, as ever.

What was I going to do? Unless Tesla could find funding, he had no recourse but to shut down Wardenclyffe and walk away. Which would leave me homeless and jobless. Would GE take me back? I didn't know. Refusing a job and then changing my mind hardly demonstrated stability.

I must have drifted off, but the kip left me unrefreshed. I returned to the ground floor and I found it empty—the workers gone, the generator gone, the same for the freight car brought in to cart it away. I didn't see Scherff, but caught the murmur of voices from Tesla's office, so I headed there.

I had just reached his door when the growing sound of a combustion engine echoed from the west side by the siding track. Curious, I made my way to the door, reaching it as the engine shut off.

Outside I found two men in an open black touring car. I did not know cars so I couldn't say what make or model. Both wore cloth caps, goggles, and dusters—all of which they set about removing as soon as they stepped out, revealing expensive three-piece suits.

The driver spotted me and said, "Tell me, young man, is Mister Tesla about?"

I nodded. "He's inside."

"Would you be so kind as to tell him Mister Rudolph Drexler wishes a word with him?"

"Do you have an appointment?" I said.

The driver looked at his passenger, staring mesmerized at the tower looming at the rear of the building. He appeared not to have heard.

The driver told me, "We have no appointment. We tried to contact his office in the city but no one answered, so we took our chances and drove out here."

"I'll see if he's available."

The driver came forward and extended a small piece of paper. "Please."

I took it. A business card:

Rudolph Drexler
Actuator
AFSO

I had no idea what *ASFO* stood for or what an "Actuator" might be, but I returned to the office door and stuck my head inside. Tesla still sat behind the desk, but he'd lifted his head from his hands now; Scherff slouched in the only other chair.

"A man named Drexler is here to see you."

Tesla frowned. "I do not know this name."

I snapped the business card down on the desktop before him. "He says he drove all the way from the city."

Tesla shook his head as he stared at the card without touching it. "I know nothing about this person. Tell him I am sorry he has traveled so far for nothing, but I wish to speak to no one."

"I believe I can change your mind about that, Herr Tesla," said a voice with a thick German accent.

I turned to see the formerly silent passenger from the car, obviously Rudolph Drexler. He looked to be in his mid-forties or approaching them. Close up his shiny black hair swept back from the widow's peak of his high forehead; bright blue eyes framed a sharp nose under dark eyebrows; thin lips and a strong chin. Despite the long trip he looked as if he'd stepped out of a dressing room with his neatly pressed checked suit and vest, complimented by a celluloid Aberdeen collar and silk tie. In one hand he carried a thick briefcase, in the other a distinctive silver headed cane wrapped in some sort of coarse black leather.

George Scherff rose to his feet saying, "Mister Tesla is not available now."

"I wish to invest in your project," Drexler said.

Tesla seemed unimpressed. "I doubt very much you can fund our needs."

Depositing his briefcase on an unopened crate, Drexler stepped forward and tapped the silver head of his cane on the desk. "I will invest whatever it takes to make this project work."

Tesla snorted. "How much do you have to spend?"

"Nein-nein, not me. Personally I am far from a rich man. But the organization I represent has impressive resources. You have my card there. Brand new, I might add. My organization made them up especially for my stay in your country."

"This AFSO?" he said, looking at the card.

"Yes. The Ancient Fraternal Septimus Order."

"I have never heard of it." He glanced at George, then me. "Either of you?"

We both shook our heads.

Drexler smiled. "We are a philanthropic organization whose members value their privacy. We aid worthy projects—ones that will move civilization forward. We seek neither profit nor adulation, and because of the desire for privacy, we work behind the scenes."

"And this 'Actuator'?" he said, tapping the card. "That is you?"

Drexler gave a short, very Prussian bow. "That is I."

"What exactly does an 'Actuator' do?"

The smile broadened. "I make things happen, so to speak. And members of the Septimus Order wish very much to see this"—he waved his cane in an all-encompassing arc—"happen."

"Why? Why not throw money at Marconi like everybody else?"

"Because we know that the Italian's success is based on your in-novations—your *patented* innovations, I might add. We know where the real brains are, and that is where we choose to invest. Besides, you have bigger dreams—not just wireless communication, but wireless energy, something we believe will completely change the world."

Hearing the echo of my own words gave me a chill. Almost as if Drexler had been eavesdropping. A ridiculous notion, I know. But still...

"I thank you for your acknowledgements," Tesla said, "and I will accept that your intentions are good. That said, I believe your organi-zation is naïve as to the enormity of the funding required here."

"Not naïve at all, Herr Tesla. We know that the estimable Herr Morgan offered you one hundred and fifty thousand dollars in ex-change for a fifty-one percent share of the patents you produced here, is that not so?"

I had no idea as to whether or not this was true, but both Tesla and Scherff looked like Drexler had thrown ice water in their faces, so I assumed Drexler was right on target.

Fifty-one percent of his patents? Nikola Tesla must have been des-perate for funding. Or, as Scherff said, no head for business. Or both.

"How...how do you know that?" Scherff said.

"The Ancient Fraternal Septimus Order is, as its name states, *an-cient*, and during the course of its lengthy existence it has gathered members from all walks of life in every country around the globe. Not much happens in this world that escapes our notice."

"But the terms of a contract," Scherff said. "How can you know—?"

"It would be much too complicated to delve into the particulars right now. Suffice it to say that we know. As we also know that Morgan has advanced only a third of what he promised. To our mind that nullifies the contract, and so I am here to offer you the one hundred thousand upon which he has reneged."

"And your terms?" Scherff said, folding his arms across his chest. "Do not expect fifty-one percent."

Tesla's vaguely sheepish look told me they'd had a major disagreement about this, and I'd wager all my savings Tesla had signed without consulting Scherff. I could see Scherff being adamantly opposed to a ridiculous figure like fifty-one percent.

"We don't expect a percentage of anything," Drexler said.

I knew I had no rightful place in this discussion but could not help blurting, "You're contributing one hundred thousand dollars and expecting nothing in return?"

"Quite the contrary, young man" Drexler said. "We are expecting Herr Tesla to change the world."

Silence followed as Drexler allowed that to sink in. After a few heartbeats, he said, "Perhaps I should add that the one hundred thousand is not the limit of our commitment. Should you need more, we shall provide it."

"Surely you will want an accounting," Scherff said.

"Of course, but we understand you gentlemen better than you think. We know dedication and scientific zeal when we see it. You have not constructed all this"—he waved his cane again—"as part of some elaborate get-rich-quick scheme. You wish to change the world as much as we."

Something about the way he said that bothered me.

And more: If he—or rather his organization—was going to fund Tesla's dream, allow it to become real, why then did he cause this uneasiness in me? A feeling somewhat akin—though nowhere near as intense—to the feeling when the tower was powered up. A vague wrongness.

He was saying all the right things. Why didn't I trust him?

"We do have one request, however."

Here it comes, I thought.

"Oh?" said Scherff. His expression told me he was thinking the same thing.

"We wish access to the designs."

"Access?" Tesla said.

"Yes. The Council would like to track your progress as things are developing. We have no interest in proprietary claims—everything is yours to patent as you wish. Once the patents are filed, the Council wishes copies for the Order's archives."

"What Council?" I said.

"The Council of Seven that oversees and guides Septimus. When you succeed, when you change the world as we know it, our involvement here will become a source of great pride."

When you succeed…as much as I mistrusted Drexler, I could not help a positive response when he said that. Not "if" but "when." The dream had risen from the dead.

I recalled Scherff's words from just a few hours ago: *The maestro always finds a way. And when he cannot, a way finds him.*

Well, it had happened. Nikola Tesla had needed financial rescue and it had walked unbidden through the door.

Tesla smoothed his mustache with a thumb and forefinger. "Copies for your archives…I don't see why not. But only after the patents have been secured. I cannot allow any plans to leave here before they are protected." He lowered his voice to a mutter. "Not that they're ever really protected."

I knew what he meant: Patents hadn't stopped Marconi.

He looked at me. "That will be your job, Charles. You can make copies for them when the proper time comes, yes?"

"Of course," I said.

Copying circuit diagrams was tedious work but I was, after all, just an apprentice.

"And one more thing," Drexler said. "The Septimus Order will want to staff a portion of your work force."

"We prefer to hire locals for unskilled and semi-skilled labor," Scherff told him. "It's more economical because we don't have to house them, and it makes for good relations with the surrounding communities. Displacing them with a crowd of outsiders might cause problems."

"I'm suggesting nothing like that. Surely you have some attrition."

"Of course. Especially now that summer is here."

"Well, then. All vacancies can be filled by skilled members of our order. We shall provide for their lodgings, of course."

"To act as spies?" Scherff said.

Drexler laughed. "Not necessary. We are already quite familiar with your operations. The same with the maestro's sojourn in Colorado Springs. Nein-nein, my friend. We do not need spies here. But our people will assure you a steady, reliable, and dedicated work force that will not be subject to the vagaries of seasonal work. They will show up every day and do exactly as they are told."

It sounded good to me. Scherff had complained of the difficulty keeping the project fully staffed through the seasons. Long Island was experiencing a boom in growth. Once the weather changed for the better, good-paying construction jobs opened all over, and the local workers flocked to them. But the decision lay with Scherff. He was in charge of operations and he did the hiring and firing.

He considered this a moment, then said, "I'd be willing to give it a trial."

"*Ausgezeichnet!* I shall set the wheels in motion as soon as I return to the city. The Council will want a formal agreement before we tender the funds, but we shall keep everything simple and above board." He raised his cane. "Now, as this is my first visit, will someone be so kind as to give me the grand tour?"

Tesla and Scherff simultaneously looked at me. They obviously had a number of matters to discuss in private.

"I will be delighted to escort you, Mister Drexler," I said with all the pleasantness I could muster.

I still did not trust this man, but I would make the best of it. During the dismantling of the generator, Scherff had dismissed most of the workers for the day, so the main floor was deserted.

When I showed him where the generator had stood, Drexler said. "Replacing that will be our first order of business."

He made appropriate appreciative noises as I showed him the

glass-blowing area, the x-ray machine, the drafting room, the stocks of wires and tubes. As I was leading him toward the rear door and the tower, he pointed to the loft.

"What is up there?"

"Just storage and my living quarters."

He stopped. "You live here?"

"I don't have much choice."

He nodded. "Yes, as an unpaid apprentice, I suppose you do not. We shall have to remedy that."

How did he know I was unpaid?

"You seem to know a lot about Wardenclyffe, sir."

A thin smile. "I have a duty to further the Septimus Order's interests, and that requires an in-depth knowledge of where to commit its resources. Such knowledge requires research. I am quite adept at research. I know all there is to know about Nikola Tesla and George Scherff. Despite my best efforts, however, you remain something of a blank."

A chill ran through me. I suddenly feared this man.

"What…" My tongue stuck to the roof of my mouth. "What could you possibly wish to know? I would think my life is an open book."

"The last five years or so, since you arrived in this country, most certainly. But before that…nothing. It is as if you winked into existence aboard the freighter that brought you here."

He was much too close to the truth. I had to derail this conversation. I forced a laugh that sounded hideous and laid on a thick layer of my native accent.

"That would be a jolly good trick, wouldn't it? But you know how things are in Blighty, don't you? Bloody halls of records burnin' down all the time, what with their bein' filled with nothin' but paper." I refrained from adding "guvna."

He looked amused. "That must be the explanation then. Whatever the case, I see you as an asset to this project and I wish you to stay on. To that end, I shall arrange a stipend for you and living quarters away from here."

That sounded wonderful but I did not want to be beholden to him.

"I'm grateful for the offer, sir, but I am fine right here."

He gave me a long look. "You are quite devoted to this project, are you not."

He made it a statement rather than a question. "Very much so."

"Very well, if you wish to live in these primitive conditions, so be it. I cannot and would not force you to change. But I can see to it that you receive a pay envelope every two weeks whether you like it or not."

I said nothing. I wasn't comfortable with it, but I certainly could use it.

"Will you at least tell me your age?"

Seeing no harm in that, I said, "Twenty-five, sir."

"That would make your birth year 1878. You are twice the age of my boy Ernst."

His tone glowed with pride in his son. I wished my father could have taken that amount of pride in me, but such was never in the cards, even if he had lived past my twelfth birthday.

"Would you like to visit the tower now?"

"Most certainly."

I held the rear door for Drexler and he, like most first timers, took two steps outside and stopped to stare up in wonder.

"I feel…" he said softly. "I feel as if I am gazing into the future. Not too long ago a countryman of yours wrote a novel about a machine that allowed one to travel forward in time. He described many wonders, but he never foresaw anything like this."

I'd heard of *The Time Machine* but hadn't had a chance to read it.

"We can climb the tower if you wish. The view is spectacular."

"I'd much prefer to plumb the depths, as it were."

I threw the switch that illuminated the shaft—at least we still had municipal power running. He left his cane leaning against one of the struts and followed me down the winding staircase.

"I am wondering," Drexler said as we descended, "why Herr Tesla did not build something like this at his lab in Colorado Springs."

"He wanted a location on the edge of the continent to begin transatlantic communications."

"Of course. That makes perfect sense."

I had no idea whether that was true or not—Tesla had never

confided in me—but it sounded logical.

At the bottom, Drexler examined the shaft, the tubing, and the tunnels, but devoted most of his attention to the recently installed Tesla coil that took up much of the space. We'd arranged the primary coil around the central shaft and buried it. The secondary coil and the doughnut-shaped toroid also encircled the shaft but were left exposed.

"This shakes the Earth?" he said.

"Not quite." Where had he got that idea? "This is a smaller version of the coil in the cupola. The whole purpose is to synchronize the natural telluric currents and create standing waves throughout the planet, thus magnifying them and allowing their capture to power lights and machinery anywhere on Earth."

"In other words, turning the Earth itself into a dynamo."

An oversimplification, but I decided not to get into the finer points.

"In a sense, yes."

"Then why the tower?"

"To broadcast energy through the air as well, allowing ships at sea and Zeppelins and other airships to power their propellers."

He smiled. "Changing the world."

"Yes, sir. That is our intent."

"Mine as well."

We made the one hundred and twenty-foot climb back to daylight. When we reached the surface, Drexler leaned against one of the tower struts, panting.

"That is quite the climb. I am unused to such exertions."

I gave him a moment to catch his breath, then gestured toward the plant. "Shall we?"

"A moment before we go back inside. Would you hand me my cane?"

I retrieved his walking stick and noticed the design atop its silver head.

"Does this have significance?" I said.

"It's the sigil of the Septimus Order."

Sept...seven point. Of course. I ran my fingers along the rough black material that encased the shaft.

"That's rhinoceros hide," he said. "My father shot the beast on safari and had the cane made to order."

"Your father belonged to this Septimus Order as well?"

"Yes. A family tradition. My boy Ernst, back in Germany with his mother, will follow in my footsteps." He retrieved the cane and waved it around. "You are aware of the recent odd occurrences in the area."

Another statement that should have been a question. I feigned ignorance.

"Whatever do you mean?"

"Come, come, Charles. You spent the morning investigating two of them." Unable to hide my shock, my expression must have looked comical, because he laughed. "I would love to play poker with you. Your face hides nothing."

If only he knew. He'd be surprised—no, *shocked*—to learn how much my face hid.

"I apologize for lacking skills in the art of deception," I said. "But…do you have spies here?"

"As I said before, the membership of the Septimus Order is widespread and varied. Now tell me: To what conclusions did your investigations lead you?"

I debated answering him. I didn't want this discussion to jeopardize his funding of the project.

As if reading my mind, he added: "I am committed to recommending that Septimus fund Herr Tesla's dream of world wireless. Nothing you say will change that. But I want your considered opinion. You have a degree in electrical engineering from a respected institution, which would suggest a logical and analytical mind, grounded in reality. So tell me: Do you detect a link between the tower and the phenomena?"

I paused to choose my words carefully.

"Well, firstly, you must realize that three incidents form an extremely limited sample."

He tapped his cane impatiently on the concrete base. "Ja-ja. That is obvious and something I already know."

"And secondly, the three phenomena in no way resemble each other. A building flaking away and vanishing into the air bears no similarity to a fish kill. Both are bizarre but both left behind concrete evidence. As for the pool incident, we have only the victim's testimony and no evidence that it ever truly happened."

"A link, Charles. Do you think there is a link?"

"The people I spoke to think so."

"*Your* opinion, Charles."

"Certainly there is a *correlation* between the incidents and the activation periods of the tower. As to whether the tower *caused* them…"

"You cannot say. I completely understand. A correlation is good enough for me."

So saying, he walked back to the plant, leaving me standing under the tower, wondering.

A correlation is good enough for me…whatever did he mean by that? *Good enough?* What *good* could he find in that sort of correlation?

OCTOBER 12, 1937

"But let's leave Wardenclyffe in the past where it belongs," Tesla said as we dominated our bench, discouraging anyone else from claiming a corner. "How is your life, Charles? What have you accomplished with all that potential?"

I thought about that. I'd often asked myself the same question.

"'Accomplished'? In objective terms, not much. In personal terms…everything."

"Everything?"

He still could not seem to take his eyes off my mustache, so I stroked it and said, "Well, I grew this." As he laughed and winced again, I added, "In all seriousness, I have managed to stay employed despite the depression. I have—"

I stopped because of the way he was staring at my mustache.

"It looks so real."

"It is." I leaned toward him. "Touch it. Go ahead."

He ran a hesitant finger over it, then snatched it away. "It *is* real!"

"I told you it was. Why are you so shocked?"

"Because all this time I thought…I thought…"

"Thought what?"

"Don't be angry with me: I thought you were a woman disguised as a man."

His words did not anger me in the least, but they certainly jolted me. Looking into his eyes I knew the time for truth had arrived.

"You're almost right. I am not a woman disguised as a man. I am a man born into a woman's body who has garbed that body to reflect my true nature."

"How…what?" Confusion reigned in his expression, and undoubtedly in his thoughts as well. "I don't understand. How does this happen?"

"I wish I knew. You want my *true* life story? I once told you I was born in Manchester in 1878—that much is true. But I was born *Charlotte* Atkinson. I had a female body but not once in my life can I remember feeling feminine or wanting to live as my mother did. I wanted my father's life. So after my mother died and I sold the cottage, I boarded a train to Liverpool as Charlotte and stepped off as Charles. You know the rest."

"But your mustache!"

Now I knew why he'd been staring. How could a woman grow a mustache?

"Testosterone," I said. "A synthesized form was developed two years ago and I've been injecting myself three times a week. I used to shave just to remove the peach fuzz. Now I *must* shave. And I love it—the favorite part of my daily ablutions."

How wonderful to reveal myself to this man I revered and owed so much.

He shook his head. "Such a challenge you set for yourself."

If he only knew…

"It isn't as if I have a choice. It is something I *must* do. I have lived my entire adult life as a man, and whatever I have accomplished in life is *because* I've lived as a man."

"You have a brilliant mind."

"I don't know about brilliant, but I know I have a good one. Yet

MIT would not have accepted me had I applied as a woman. They accepted a rare woman back then, but only if she could live nearby with her family. As a female orphan from England, I'd have been rejected out of hand, despite my high test score. Remember, women didn't even have the right to vote until 1920. And you—would you have taken me on if I'd approached you as a woman?"

He shook his head. "Of course not. I have always thought women the intellectual equals of men and that they would someday startle the world with their innovations. But the presence of a woman would have been a terrible distraction to the workers, catastrophically disruptive."

Something didn't fit here...

"When did you discover my secret?"

"During your first year."

So early?

"How?"

"I went to your quarters in the loft to see if we might make you more comfortable. I found a bloody rag."

"Ah...my monthly." The bane of my transformation.

"I didn't know that then. I thought you might have cut yourself. But there was so much blood...and your face was so hairless...I began to keep track of the times you didn't look well, and then I would check, and I'd find blood."

I'd worked so hard at hiding my monthlies. I might have been a man in a woman's body, but a woman's body has undeniable and indomitable rhythms, irrespective of the soul inhabiting it. At age fifty-nine now, they are a thing of the past, but back then I had to sneak out at night once a month and bury the bloody rags in the field far beyond the tower. Some of those nights were bitter cold and the ground hard as stone.

"So if you knew," I said, "why didn't you sack me?"

He gave one of his Serbian shrugs. "You may deny your brilliance, but I do not. In everyone's eyes you were a man—a very boyish looking man, yes, but you *functioned* as a man. That made all the difference. As a woman among them, you would distract the workers; they would look at you and think of sex instead of their tasks. They'd be posturing instead of working. But day to day they looked upon you as a man and so you caused no disruption. As for myself, I was and am celibate, so the truth did not affect me."

"Weren't you angry that I'd deceived you?"

He gave a short laugh. "I suppose I was too confused to be angry. I did not understand the how nor the why of the way you were living— and I still do not—but I had come to know you and like you and trust you. I knew you truly shared my dream. I wanted to keep you for your mind and your enthusiasm and your dedication, but mostly because I did not want to crush your dream of being a part of worldwide wireless. So I decided I would keep your secret and that you would stay."

I blinked away tears that threatened to spill. I loved this man.

"You kept the secret extremely well," I said, my voice wobbling. "I shall forever revere you for that."

Never comfortable with emotion, he waved off my gratitude. "You deserve all you've achieved."

I hadn't told him the rest of it.

"You didn't let me finish before. I have a wife and a daughter—"

Eyes wide, he grabbed my forearm. "A child? But how?"

"I married a wonderful woman. I love her and she loves me. No more need be said. Our daughter was adopted as an infant and we treasure her. I am, in every sense, the Man of the House."

Yes…a very unconventional man living a very conventional life.

He slapped his thighs. "Well then, you have answered my question. You have gotten what you wanted from life."

"Except world wireless."

He sighed. "Yes. Except that."

"And so I rest my case and say again: Whatever I have accomplished in life is because I've lived as a man. To which I must add: And because I met you."

"But then," he said with a frown, "had you not met me, you would have been spared the horrors of Wardenclyffe."

I could not argue with that…

1904

We accomplished very little for the remainder of the year and not until spring did we finally have the new generator installed and running. Much of the early delays involved the Septimus Order. Apparently, despite Drexler's enthusiastic endorsement, not all of the Council of Seven supported the idea of risking such a huge amount of money on an unproven technology. At least that was how Drexler explained the delay to us. I had a feeling it went deeper.

He would train Council members out to Wardenclyffe to see the tower and the shaft first hand. Invariably I was tasked with conducting the tour. And there I became aware of a puzzling trend: the Council members seemed more interested in the anomalous phenomena that correlated to activating the tower than the possibilities inherent in worldwide wireless.

A number of them wished for a demonstration of the tower before committing to the investment, but without their investment we had no generator, and without a generator we could demonstrate nothing.

Finally wiser heads prevailed and Drexler announced that the money was ready to flow as soon as Tesla signed a "simple and straightforward" formal agreement. A major sticking point turned out to be the Council's insistence that all funds flow through Drexler. This naturally upset George Scherff who had functioned for years as Tesla's accountant and bookkeeper. Drexler apologized but said the Council had been firm on this point because it allowed them to monitor expenditures. Scherff wasn't cut out entirely: He would receive a lump sum every week to cover payroll.

On and on it went, one delay after another, bogged in minutiae like property taxes and such. After much searching about we secured a generator with the power Tesla required. We repaired the relationship with the coal supplier and fired her up. All connections had to be retested. Once that was done, we were ready for a low-wattage experimental run.

In all that time, I held to a careful routine that would keep me useful and yet unobtrusive. Since boarding the freighter in Liverpool, I had pitched my voice low until it became second nature to me. I'd also perfected my breast-binding technique until I could do it quickly, without thinking. Fortunately I had a slim build and was anything but busty. But I always made sure my shirts were loose fitting, and I dressed in multiple layers when I could—easy enough in the winter but a constant challenge in the warmer months. I wished for a way to permanently remove them but that was not an option.

I was forever on guard against a slip. For years now the story of Murray Hall had haunted me. The scandal had broken in 1901 when I was still at MIT. A fixture in New York's Tammany Hall politics for a quarter century, Murray Hall was discovered upon his death to be a woman. How humiliating. Was that the fate that awaited me?

A nationwide uproar followed. After all, women weren't even allowed to vote, let alone have a say in a powerful political machine. Born Mary Anderson in Scotland, she'd arrived in America wearing her dead brother's clothes.

The parallels terrified me. I could not afford a slip-up. I needed Wardenclyffe. I *belonged* here…

…because I belonged nowhere else.

At night, as I lay awake waiting for sleep, when I wasn't worrying about exposure, I worried about my future. After Wardenclyffe, whether we succeeded or failed, what lay ahead for me? Would I ever find someone who could accept me as I am, who would stand by me and allow me to be me? I could weather the loneliness and isolation now, but not forever. I would need someone to share my life and I'd begun to despair of ever finding that someone.

The challenge of changing the world would be my companion for now. And all Wardenclyffe needed to get back into gear was a foggy day—plentiful in spring, summer, and fall, but not so much in winter.

"I don't see why we have to wait," Drexler said for perhaps the hundredth time.

He had become a fixture at the plant, spending many of his days here. He'd done away with his driver and taken over the wheel of his four-seater touring car, ferrying Tesla, Scherff, and himself back and forth from their Port Jefferson quarters.

And for perhaps the hundredth time, George Scherff explained that a nighttime display attracted too much attention—the flashes were visible up and down the Sound, and all the way across to New Haven and Bridgeport.

"What's wrong with attention?" Drexler said.

"The displays frighten people," Scherff told him. "And frightened people do not act rationally. They might shut us down. Do you want that?"

Of course he didn't. But that wouldn't stop him from asking again before too long.

Eventually a warm front pushed through, and by ten A.M. on March 9, 1904, nature provided us the means to muffle the tower's flashes.

The workers were given the day off. Drexler insisted on being present. And how could anyone say no? None of this would be happening without him.

This time, I was assigned the task of throwing the switch. When I reached the others standing by the rear door, the show had already begun. The cupola was lost to view in the fog above but blue-white light flashes lit the mist. The shaft was flashing, too, with discharges from the Tesla coil below.

Tesla picked up a ceramic cylinder with a fifty-watt light bulb attached to one end and two copper prongs protruding from the other. A small induction coil connected them in the center. I'd helped put it together.

He waited to let the tower warm up a little more, then walked to a patch of dead grass off to the left and stuck the pair of prongs into the ground. He stepped back and we all watched.

Slowly, the filament inside the bulb began to glow, growing brighter and brighter until fully lit.

Drexler watched slack jawed while Tesla only smiled and nodded—he'd seen this before. Not so Scherff and I, however, and the two of us clapped and laughed. I was so filled with wonder and delight that I had to rush back inside to hide sudden tears.

It worked, it worked, it *worked*!

"Very well," Tesla said. "This is a low-power experiment. Let us see how far we can go."

I'd composed myself by then, so I hurried outside. I knew what was expected of me.

I plucked the makeshift light fixture from the ground and started walking toward the tower. I held it aloft, watching the bulb to see if it might begin to glow but knowing it would not. It had not been designed for aerial reception. Still, one could always hope.

I held it high with no result until I'd passed the tower, then dropped it to my side and kept walking. When I'd gone exactly fifty paces, I stopped and looked back. I could still see a vague outline of the base of the tower, and faint flashes above and from below. But the plant beyond had been swallowed entirely.

I thrust the prongs into the ground and waited. Once again the filament glowed and the bulb lit to full power. I pulled out a pea whistle and blew it. Seemingly out of nowhere came an echoing response from Scherff's whistle.

Plucking the bulb from the ground, I walked on and soon was moving through a featureless gray limbo. The sun was shining somewhere above but you couldn't prove it by me. The tower had disappeared behind, and only blank mist lay ahead. It didn't bother me.

Well, perhaps a little. I made monthly trips out here in the dark with a spade to bury my bloody rags, but at least then I could use a light in one of the plant windows to guide me back. Right now I could not be sure of my direction. I assumed I was traveling north toward the Sound, but that was merely an assumption.

Another fifty paces and I stopped for another test of the bulb. Once again it lit. I blew my whistle and waited for Scherff's response. And waited. Hearing nothing, I blew again. Still no response, so I blew as hard as I could. Nothing.

Was all the moisture in the air swallowing the sound?

No matter, really. We'd anticipated some of these difficulties in the fog, and so the plan was for me to keep walking and testing until the bulb stopped lighting or until I reached the Sound. If the former, I was to leave the bulb where it failed to glow, and we'd take measurements after the weather cleared. If the latter, I was to turn around and make my way back.

Another fifty paces, another ground insertion, another light up. I went on and on, repeating the procedure again and again. The tower was operating on low power and yet look how far I'd come with no sign of weakening. Despite the lack of response, I dutifully blew the whistle each time. But the last time I blew it, the blast of a bloody foghorn damn near knocked me off my feet. Although it echoed from all over, it seemed to have originated behind me.

I stalked in that direction and within twenty paces reached the waterline.

Above, the fog still blocked the sun, but down at the surface of the Sound the mist had broken into drifting bands of gray. I saw a trawler steaming west from the Atlantic, smoke pouring from her stack as she headed home from deep-sea fishing. As it chugged into a particularly thick bank, a crewman spotted me and waved. I waved back just before the fog closed around it.

As it disappeared from sight an unusual churning disturbed the surface. I thought it might be the trawler's wake but instead of dissipating it increased in violence.

A scream from the fog startled me. A man's scream—whether pain or terror I couldn't tell. Perhaps both.

And then something cold and wet slammed against my chest, knocking me back. And then again—another! All around me fish were leaping from the water to land on the sand and flop around. For a moment it seemed to be raining fish. And then, just as suddenly as it had started, it stopped.

I stood at the waterline, gasping, shaking. The turbulence had died. And the boat, the trawler…where was it? It never emerged from the fog bank. Even if I couldn't see the boat itself, it would be leaving a wake. Yet the surface lay as smooth and still as a mirror.

I shook off my paralysis and began tossing the stranded fish back into the water, but gave up after a while. Too bloody many of them.

The old Gypsy woman's words came back to me then:

"You are thinking fish leaping toward *something? Look again. See how far they jump—even bottom dwellers. No, were running* from *something… Something scare fish—scare so much are leaping onto dry land to escape."*

Suddenly I wanted away from the water—*needed* to be away. So quiet, but the memory of that scream haunted me. The water…peaceful now…on the surface. But beneath…something in the depths had stirred.

My brain churned as I hurried away. Had the standing waves the tower generated in the Earth awakened something? But how would that be related to the disappearance of the barn? I could find no consistency, no pattern other than the operation of the tower. But if the tower were the cause, why then didn't the fish flee the water every time we powered it up?

I spotted the bulb fixture ahead, still glowing. I snatched it from the ground and began to run back toward the tower…or rather where I thought it would be.

I passed through a particularly thick band of fog and when I broke free the ground had changed. Instead of level, it sloped upward, and the familiar scraggly weeds and scrub had changed to oddly shaped plants with undulating tendrils instead of leaves, and flowers that seemed to open and close like mouths.

I shook my head to clear it just as I entered another thickened fog band. When I broke free the vegetation had returned to the familiar, but I still couldn't see the tower. It should have been straight ahead... at least I *hoped* it was.

What if the tower and plant were no longer there? What if they'd vanished and I was stranded in some strange, mysterious landscape. What if—?

Where were these thoughts coming from? This wasn't like me. Before leaving England I'd read Machen's wildly reviled *The Great God Pan*—precisely because it had been so vociferously denounced—and couldn't help feeling how this inexplicable, daytime nightmare might have been pulled from its pages.

And then, ahead and slightly to the left, I saw flashes high in the fog—the tower's cupola. The burst of relief annoyed me—no, *angered* me. I was a sane, rational man, trained in a logical science. Everything had an explanation. All one need do was gather the facts. The fantastic had no place in my life.

And yet, for a moment there, my disorientation in the fog had allowed my imagination to get the better of me. At least I hoped it had been my imagination.

When I reached the tower and the plant, I barely broke stride as I ran inside and turned off the generator. Tesla rushed out of his office.

"What are you doing? What is the meaning of this?"

Panting from the run, I turned to him and said, "We have to talk."

* * *

I convinced them all—Tesla, Scherff, and Drexler—to gather in the office and hear me out. I told them about the second fish kill and the disappearing boat. And the scream. I left out the irrational fear that for a short while I'd been somewhere other than Wardenclyffe. The feeling had lasted only a moment.

I also related the gist of my conversations with Mr. Herring and Mrs. Williams. Drexler had already heard this, but it was news to Tesla and Scherff, and they seemed dumbfounded. Drexler, on the other hand, seemed excited.

He went to the window. "The fog's lifting. If you fellows don't mind, I'm going down to the water for a look."

No one objected.

As Drexler pulled on his suit jacket and headed for the office door, I turned to Tesla: "What was it that woman said to you last year after the first fish kill? And please don't dismiss it as 'nonsense' again, because we have another load of dead fish out there."

He frowned. "What woman?"

"Surely you remember. The Gypsy woman who spoke to you in Serbian. The one with the dog."

Drexler skidded to a stop in the doorway. "Dog? A woman with a dog? What *did* she say?"

"Some nonsense about a wall."

"She mentioned a *wall?*" Drexler seemed to have forgotten about the dead fish. "You're sure she said 'wall'?"

Why is this so important to him? I wondered.

"Yes. She used the word *zid*—wall. She said, 'You must stop what you are doing. You made a crack in the wall. If you keep it up the crack will become a hole.' Obviously she is crazy. There was not a wall in sight."

"She is most crazy," Drexler said. "*Verrückt!*"

"You know her?" I said.

"I know *of* her. A meddlesome *schlampe.*"

I had no idea what that meant but it hardly sounded complimentary.

I said, "She was a random woman walking down the bloody beach. How could you possibly think it's the same one you know?"

"Because that sounds exactly like something she would say. And she is never without a dog. Always a dog."

"You seem…afraid of her," I said.

"What? Nein. Not at all." Pointing to each of us in turn, he said, "I am afraid for you and you and you!"

"She looked quite harmless," Scherff said.

"She will not hurt your body." He jabbed a finger against his temple. "She will hurt you *here*. Poison your *mind.*"

He looked a little mad at that moment. And he feared her, of that I had no doubt.

"Poison against what?" I said.

"Changing the world! Some people do not want change. They want everything like it always was. If you see her again, avoid her. Do not listen." The finger against his skull again. "Poison!" He stepped back toward the door. "And now I go to see the dead fish."

The three of us stood silent for a moment after he'd gone. Finally I turned to Tesla and arched an eyebrow.

"I do believe you upset him."

My understatement was lost on him. "I am not concerned with Mister Drexler's upsetment. *I* am upset. I believe we all should be upset. We have unexplained phenomena we must deal with."

"We can deal with them some other time," Scherff said. "The important thing we seem to be losing sight of is that the experiment was a success! The bulb lit when we stuck it into the ground. It is a miracle!"

"A 'miracle'?" Tesla gave him a withering look. "It is nothing of the sort. It is simply more experimental proof of my theories. I already did this in Colorado Springs." He looked from Scherff to me, pain in his eyes. I could see that this man, who eschewed emotion in everything he did, felt hurt, betrayed by his closest associates. "The two of you—did you think I made it up?"

"No-no," Scherff said. "It's just that..." He looked to me for help, a plea in his eyes.

"Nothing of the sort, sir," I blurted. "It's...it's like being told that two men have built a motor-driven machine that flies—like the Wright brothers just last December." The papers had been delirious with the news at the time. "Hearing about it, believing it's true, can't compare to what it must have been like to stand on that beach and watch it happen."

I was reaching, desperately making this up as I went along. Not just for Scherff, but for myself as well. Perhaps in my heart of hearts I hadn't truly believed that wireless energy was possible. If so, I'd been betraying Nikola Tesla on a daily basis. How else to explain the flood of conflicting emotions earlier when I'd seen that light bulb start to glow after being stuck in the ground?

In the ground!

He nodded, seemingly satisfied. "I understand."

Scherff threw me a grateful look as he said, "We must push the experiment further—test the limits of the tower's range."

"But what of the fish kills?" I said. "And the barn?"

Tesla shrugged. "We will investigate as best we can, but when the next fog comes, we will act." He pointed to me. "I want you to go down to the waterline every day and check for stranded fish. If you find none each day and then they mysteriously reappear after our next test, I will concede that we might well have a cause-effect relationship that must be explored. But until then, it is mere anecdote."

In a way, I understood that. What could make a barn disappear? And how could you relate it to the tower? As for the trawler today? Scream or no scream, probability said it had not vanished from existence, merely from sight. Odds were good that it was tied up at a fishery dock now, unloading its catch.

But I could not ignore the fact that Nikola Tesla was attempting something unique in the history of the race—in the history of the *planet*. Something unprecedented. And without precedent, where were the reference points?

* * *

Days passed without fog but we put them to good use. I did my waterline reconnoiter every morning, hoping to come upon more dead fish but finding none. Just one fish kill unrelated to the tower would be enough to break the correlation, but no such luck.

Recurrent articles appeared in the local paper about a missing trawler, the *Brinicombe*, due back in port on the day of our last test. It had been spotted passing Orient Point just before the fog settled in, and never seen again. Three days now and no sign of it. Was the *Brinicombe* the trawler that had passed? I hadn't seen its transom, so I had no idea of its name.

On the twelfth, Drexler and I rode up the coast in his car, looking for places to start testing the bulb fixture during our next run.

Right after the last test Drexler had brought in three members of his Septimus group to replace some of the locals lost by attrition. For some reason I'd expected them to be German like Drexler but they turned out to be born and bred Americans. The three were around my age and good workers who kept pretty much to themselves. As I tended to do the same, I did not get to know them beyond a nodding basis.

Tesla wanted to start testing the bulb far from the tower—find a spot between thirty and forty miles away, he told us. I thought he was going to extremes, but who was I to argue?

His plan was to start at a far distance and move in, rather than start close and move outward. It made sense in a way. If the bulb lit at the extreme distance, the experiment could be called a success and halted right then and there. If not, the plan was to drive the bulb five miles closer to the tower and try again.

The coastline to the west was too populated for our purposes, so Drexler drove us east along the peninsula known as the North Fork. The black touring car had a surrey roof and was called a "Cadillac." We had the only mechanized vehicle in evidence on our trip along North Road. We encountered plenty of horse-drawn vehicles, though. The Cadillac's loud internal combustion engine scared a lot of the horses and caused the local ladies to cover their ears as we passed.

When the odometer indicated thirty-four miles we found ourselves outside Greenport Village, near the end of the fork and the last stop on the Long Island Railroad.

"This meets the distance requirement," I said.

The village itself sat on what the locals called the Peconic River but did not look at all like a river. Whatever it was, the locale wasn't suitable for the experiment, especially with the attention the Cadillac drew. No one who came near it could resist touching it. So we headed north to the ocean side and found a beach that perfectly suited our needs.

"This is where you'll do your first planting," Drexler said with a grin. "Like tulips, ja? You plant a bulb and hope for a bright flower."

I grasped the image. Not terribly apt but I smiled and nodded to show appreciation of his attempt at wit.

"And should it not light," I said, "where will we try next? I saw a sign for something called the Horton Point Lighthouse a few miles back. That could be our second spot."

"Not 'our' spot," he said. "*Yours*. You will be on your own."

What was he saying?

"But I can't get out here by myself. Who'll drive me?"

Another grin, tighter this time. "You will."

"I've never—"

"I am going to teach you. Now."

"But why?"

"Because I need to be at the tower when the power goes on."

"You've no electrical training. Tesla doesn't need you there."

"You must learn to listen more closely: *I* need to be there. I must bear witness."

"Witness? To what?"

"Anything that happens."

"For whom?"

"For the Council. And for myself." He slid out of the car and indicated the driver seat. "*Bitte*."

I had no desire to drive a car. I couldn't see that I'd ever own one, so why should I learn to drive?

"That's not necessary," I said.

"If you don't learn to drive, you will not be able to perform your part of the experiment."

Well, put that way…how could I say no?

And so I learned to drive.

* * *

"What if the first fog comes at night?" I said on the morning of the Ides of March.

The four of us filled Tesla's office. The question had occurred to me during today's driving lesson. The mere thought of traveling North Road with all possible speed in the fog had my nerves on edge. But in the fog after dark?

"I do not see what difference it will make," Tesla said. "If it is sufficiently thick to muffle the flashes, we will proceed with the test run. We must take advantage of every opportunity."

"It will make a difference in how fast I can travel," I said. "It might take me hours to reach Greenport in the dark and fog." I looked at Drexler. "How long will your headlights burn?"

He frowned. "The boy has a point. Once the kerosene runs out, he will be lost in the dark."

Scherff said, "We need a contingency plan. What if you select a second site perhaps ten miles from the tower? Let that be your goal if you must travel at night, and keep Greenport as your daytime destination."

Ten miles…less than a third of the distance to Greenport. That sounded good to me.

* * *

Toward sunset on the eve of the first day of spring, a thick fog bank started rolling in off the Atlantic.

I threw on an oilskin and rushed to the car with Drexler behind me. I'd been practicing and had taken it out for short runs on my own, but here I faced the longest trip of my life. We'd kept the tank full of petroleum distillate in anticipation of this moment.

"Now remember your lessons," he said. "I'll help you get it started."

I got behind the wheel, made sure the gear was in neutral, and set the throttle. Drexler turned the crank and the engine exploded to life. While the engine warmed, Drexler and I lit the kerosene headlamps—I'd need them in the foggy dark. When the engine was ready, I donned a cap and goggles, then used the left pedal to put it into low gear and get moving. Once rolling, I let out the pedal to allow it to pass through neutral and into high gear—the car had only two.

I was on my way.

So much depended on me that it took all my will not to vomit.

I kept the throttle as open as I dared. I knew a swift horse could probably run faster but I felt as if I were flying. And that might have been a pleasant sensation if not for the fog blowing in my face. I had to wipe at my goggles constantly with one of the rags I'd brought along. The surrey top offered little protection and the open interior of the car was soon dripping moisture. At least the rest of me was warm and dry within the oilskin.

I was fortunate too that the fog had chosen to visit on a Sunday evening, because I had North Road quite literally to myself. A good thing too, because with the fall of night and the thickening of the fog, my world shrank to the small, misty stretch of road directly before my headlamps. My greatest fear was a deer crossing my path. I'd have no warning and if I struck it my lamps would surely be damaged, and then what would I do?

But the fog seemed to be keeping the deer off the road as well. At least I wouldn't need to endure this all the way to Greenport. Earlier in the week we'd chosen an area ten miles up the coast called Baiting Hollow, just north of the town of Riverhead.

I couldn't see the odometer so I had to depend on the crude road sign I'd chosen as my landmark. I almost missed it, and if the fog had been just a little thicker, I might have sailed right past. But I caught the word "Riverhead" out of the corner of my eye and braked to a halt.

I looked around but couldn't recognize the side road we'd used to find our way to the Baiting Hollow beach. I didn't need the beach. All I needed was a patch of earth.

I hopped out with the bulb fixture and jabbed its prongs into the ground.

"Please work," I whispered. I wanted out of this car and off this road, but most of all I wanted proof that I could find enough current ten miles from the tower to light this bulb. "Please, please, *please* work."

I stared at the filament—or rather where I assumed the filament to be since I couldn't see a bloody thing—and willed it to glow. Then, wonder of wonders, it obeyed my command. A faint ruddiness brightened to an orange line and then the bulb was glowing in all its fifty-watt splendor. The tower, ten miles away, was feeding this lonely lightbulb!

I screamed with boundless joy.

And, I confess, no little relief.

Grabbing the fixture, I leaped into the idling Cadillac and turned it around. The trip back seemed shorter—just as wet and nerve-wracking, but blessedly shorter. I expected everyone to be waiting for me with anxious anticipation.

Instead I found horror and chaos.

* * *

The tower's cupola was flashing dimly through the fog as I approached, but it stopped just as I pulled up by the railroad siding. I ran in, ready to shout the good news, but stumbled to a halt at the sight of a man lying on the floor in a pool of blood. One of Drexler's recruits—face deathly white, mouth agape, eyes open and staring, and a ragged bloody hole where his throat should have been.

My stomach clenched. So much blood. Why would someone cut his throat? A fight? But his throat wasn't simply slashed—it had been torn out.

I dragged my stunned and horrified gaze from him to take in the rest of the interior. George Scherff stood by the door to Tesla's office, a two-by-four raised like a cricket bat, ready for a swing.

The two other Septimus hires also carried lengths of lumber, but weren't squaring off against each other or against Scherff. They appeared to be scanning the air around them, as if expecting an attack from above.

Beyond them, at the far end by the generator room, stood Tesla, his hand on the power lever and a terrified expression on his face.

And then Drexler ran in from the rear waving a pistol—a pistol!

"They're coming back!" he shouted.

Who was coming back?

I ran to Scherff. "George! What's happ—?"

His eyes widened as he saw me. "Charles! Into the office!" He reached behind him for the doorknob. "Quickly!"

I stopped. I wasn't going anywhere until I knew what was happening. I certainly wasn't going to let him protect me like I was some helpless woman. I was neither.

"Why? What's—?"

"We're under attack! Now get—"

"By whom? Locals?"

"No." He dropped into a crouch and pointed up. "Them!"

At first I didn't know what he meant, then movement in the air a dozen feet off the ground caught my eye.

"Bloody hell!"

Winged things—three of them—that might have escaped one of Doré's visions of hell. Roughly the size of large lobsters with shelled bodies and numerous dangling claws, but these had narrow waists like wasps and were held aloft by diaphanous dragonfly wings, blurred by the speed of their beating. But neither lobsters nor wasps had teeth, and certainly nothing ever born on Earth had teeth like these—wide, drop-hinge jaws packed with long, sharp, transparent fangs like diamond stilettos.

I instantly surmised what had befallen the dead man's throat.

What were these things? I might have wondered where they'd come from, but had a sickening feeling I already knew.

The three creatures diverged and dove to the attack—two angling toward Drexler and his men, the other toward George and me.

Drexler shouted, "Cover me!"

He was fiddling with some wood contraption, trying to attach it to the whiskbroom handle of his pistol as he backed toward the surviving Septimus members. In response, they stepped forward and began swinging their two-by-fours at the monsters.

I lost interest in their plight when I realized the remaining monster was headed straight for me. I dropped to the floor as it zoomed above with an angry buzz. It overshot me but quickly banked around and came in for another pass.

Scherff was shouting something I couldn't understand while I looked frantically about for something to use against it. I spotted a metal strut on the floor about twenty feet away. Staying in a crouch, I made a dash for it but the angry buzzing grew so loud behind me I feared the thing was almost upon me, so I threw myself flat on the floor.

As it came around for another run, I had an idea. Jumping up, I raced back toward Scherff.

"You can't outrun it!" he shouted.

"I know! I'm bringing it to you! Get ready!"

I hoped he understood, and when he raised the lumber in a two-handed grip, I knew he did.

The buzzing grew louder and louder behind me. I feared I'd feel those teeth in my nape any second. As I reached Scherff I dropped into a slide, leaving him with a clear shot at the thing.

"Don't miss!" I cried.

I didn't see him swing but a loud *crunch!* and the sudden cessation of the buzzing told me he'd connected. I rolled to my feet and turned to see him pounding the monstrous thing again and again as it flopped and fluttered on the ground.

Beyond him, Drexler had fitted a stock to the grip of his pistol, transforming it into a kind of short-barreled rifle. As I watched, he dropped to one knee, raised it to his shoulder, and took aim at the two remaining creatures.

His first shot made an impressive *crack!* that echoed through the interior but missed both. With his second shot, one of the things flipped in the air and went into a descending spiral. When it hit the ground, one of the Septimus men ran toward it with his club raised. He made the mistake of taking his eyes off the remaining creature, which went into a dive toward him. He shouted with shock and pain as it sank its dagger teeth into his upper thigh. Blood gushed from the wound as the thing tore out a chunk of flesh.

Before it could fly off, however, his Septimus companion arrived to smash it to the ground. And while he clubbed it to death, Drexler stepped up and administered a coup de grâce to the toothy head of the one he'd wounded.

And then...silence.

We all stood where we were, doing slow turns as we searched the air for further threats.

"Are there more?" I finally said.

"No," Scherff said with a quick shake of his head. "At least I hope not. I saw three come out of the shaft and—"

"The *shaft*? How did they get into the shaft?"

"That is what I would like to know. I was out there with Rourke"— he indicated the dead man—"when we saw these three things rise through all the flashings from below and hover around the pipe. When we stepped forward for a closer look, they came at us and we ran. We managed to close the rear door to keep them out, but the side door was open. We ran to shut it but one of them caught Rourke before we could reach it."

Tesla joined the group after a slow, hesitant trip from the far side of the workspace. His slack expression indicated shock.

The wounded Septimus worker dropped to his knees then, clutching his bloody thigh. His companion helped him up and supported him as he limped back toward the first aid room.

Drexler took up the story.

"I unwittingly opened the rear doors, allowing two of them in. They buzzed around and appeared to leave, but came back before I could close the door again." He waved the pistol. "I ran and got this."

"You carry a pistol?" I said.

"In my briefcase always. Good thing too, ja?"

I had to agree. "Ja."

I walked over to the thing Drexler had killed. A bullet had pierced its waist area and the coup de grâce had blown away the upper part of its head, but it had the least overall damage compared to the victims of the two-by-fours. Close up now I could see a string of bioluminescent dots running along its flank, still glowing faintly, even in death.

But the teeth…those teeth held my attention. I'd seen drawings of piranha fish from the Amazon and had thought they looked like perfect killing machines, but this creature left them in the dust. And it could fly. If you want safety from a piranha, stay out of the water. Where was safe from this thing?

Tesla, Scherff, and Drexler joined me as I squatted next to it.

I said, "Does anyone have any idea where these things came from and how they got into the tower shaft?"

"I never saw them go in," Scherff said. "I only saw them come out."

"But they had to go in," I said. "You and I have been down there hundreds of times. We've seen common everyday beetles and such, but never—"

"They came through the wall," Tesla said.

We all stared at him. He did not look well. His eyes lacked their usual focus.

I said, "The wall of the shaft, sir?"

"The wall I was warned about," he said in a flat tone. "The one the woman said I was cracking."

Drexler's sudden laugh sounded forced. "That crazy Gypsy you told me about? Such silliness. I have my own theory about these things and it has nothing to do with a crack in a wall that isn't here in the first place."

"I wish to hear this," Scherff said.

Drexler began slowly, as if gathering his thoughts. "Well, you have heard of dinosaurs, ja?" When we all nodded, he went on. "And so we have seen the drawings of the skeletons of the flying dinosaurs, ja?"

"Pterosaurs," I said.

Dinosaurs had always fascinated me. I was well aware we were not terribly far from the site where the Haddon hadrosaurus had been discovered.

"Ja, pterosaurs," Drexler said with growing excitement. "I believe you are right about the name. I am wondering whether it is possible that we have before us prehistoric creatures, left over from the days of the dinosaurs, that were trapped in the soil around the shaft. Could it be that all the electric discharges from the coil at the bottom of the shaft awoke them? And, once awake, they flew up the shaft to appear in the modern world. Naturally, being predators—considering those teeth, what else could they be?—they attacked the nearest food: us."

"If you're right," I said, "then we've discovered a new prehistoric species."

Reanimated prehistoric creatures…a fantastical concept, yet one I found more easily acceptable than a crack in an even more fantastical invisible wall.

"I am sure I am right," Drexler said. "And to prove it, we must take these to an expert on prehistoric creatures."

"Where would one find such a person?" Scherff said.

Drexler shrugged. "I am only a visitor in this land. I do not know these things. But you must have someplace."

I had an idea for that. "The Museum of Natural History in New York City. If anyone can identify this monster, you will find him there."

"Yes!" Drexler slammed a fist into his palm. He had passed beyond excitement into some strange exalted state. "Then that is where

I shall take them. Help Herr Tesla back to his office while I prepare these for transport to the city."

Tesla didn't need help, merely guidance. He still seemed dazed by the incident. As I led him toward his office, Scherff said, "What about Rourke here? We'll have to call the authorities."

Oh, yes. The poor dead man. The fight for our lives had pushed his tragedy into the background.

"Nein-nein!" Drexler said. "We shall handle it. Septimus takes care of its own."

Scherff was shaking his head. "I do not know if that is a good idea. We could be in trouble."

I motioned Scherff to follow me into the office. He arrived as I was guiding Tesla into his desk chair.

"I think Drexler is right," I said in a low voice. "If we report Rourke's death, we will have to show those things as the cause of death. How do we explain them without risking a panic? If people hear that the tower is reanimating prehistoric creatures…"

Scherff had started nodding so I stopped there.

"I see, I see. We will let Drexler handle the body and the beasts then."

"The beasts," Tesla said in a flat tone. "I breached the wall and let them through."

"No, maestro," Scherff said. "That was just a crazy woman talking."

The wall…I couldn't help hearkening back to the Machen story and its poor woman who had a glimpse of the "spiritual world" and lost her mind. I couldn't accept that those creatures had come through a breach in an invisible wall between our existence and another. And even though Drexler's theory sounded preposterous as well, it seemed less so.

I tried to focus Tesla on some good news: "I never got to tell you both that the experiment was a resounding success. The bulb lit at the ten-mile mark."

"But we breached the wall in the process," Tesla droned.

Scherff turned to me. "He's in shock. He'll come around."

Yes, he would. But not before the horrors multiplied to an unimaginable degree.

By Wednesday we'd had no word from Drexler and I was growing impatient.

He, along with the three Septimus men—two living, one dead—and the remains of the creatures, had departed under cover of night as soon as the fog lifted.

I'd checked the waterline the next morning and was heartened to find no dead fish.

Tesla improved overnight but was not quite himself. He deserted Wardenclyffe to recover in comfort in his Waldorf Astoria quarters. And George Scherff…well, Scherff was his practical Teutonic self, keeping everything up and running in the maestro's absence.

The big question, which no one was addressing yet, was whether or not we should continue the experiments. By some unspoken agreement, Scherff and I did not bring it up between us, even for idle discussion. After all, the decision was not ours. We needed Tesla to return to Wardenclyffe as his old self.

With everything in limbo, and finding myself at sixes and sevens, I decided to call the Natural History Museum. I was burning with curiosity about the identity of those creatures and the prehistoric era that had spawned them.

Since Tesla's office was not in use, I used the phone there to call. I had visited the museum twice since my arrival from Boston, and found it fascinating. Upon reaching the switchboard I asked the operator to connect me with anyone in paleontology. The man who answered had no idea what I was talking about. No, they had received no prehistoric specimens from Long Island or anywhere else this week. When I told him they had been alive on Sunday and that these could be the find of the century, he became angry, saying he had no patience for hoaxes nor those who perpetrated them, and hung up.

His anger had seemed genuine, lending credence to his denial. No question that the arrival of specimens such as the creatures that had attacked us would have caused quite a stir at the museum. Even the lowest secretary would have been aware of this sort of find.

Which told me that Herr Drexler had not turned them over to the museum. At least not yet. What could have delayed him? They would be decomposing by now.

I opened the broad middle drawer of Tesla's desk and quickly found Drexler's card. *ASFO…Actuator…*no telephone number but, along the bottom, a New York City address.

I pocketed the card and headed for my quarters in the loft. With the maestro gone, Scherff could manage quite well without me. As for Herr Rudolph Drexler…he was going to have a visitor, one in search of an explanation as to why he had reneged on his promise to deliver the specimens to the museum.

* * *

Dressed in my suit and derby, I trained into Long Island City and took the side-wheeler ferry across to Manhattan. I'd read that workers had started tunneling under the East River to provide train access directly into the city, but that project was years from completion. I found a map of Manhattan posted on one of the ferry's inside walls. After a squinting search that made my eyes ache, I found Drexler's street on the Lower East Side. The ferry would drop me off up on 34th Street, but the morning was cool and crisp and I didn't mind a two-mile walk after so much sitting.

I'd spent the past nine months in Wardenclyffe breathing the sea air from the Sound and the pine scents from the land. As a result, the stench of the city came as an olfactory assault. Yes, I was walking down Manhattan's First Avenue, but I might as well have been standing in a stable. Horse-drawn hansoms, barouches, calashes, carts, and lorries everywhere, and every horse leaving piles of manure in its wake. Boston had been the same during my time there, I'm sure, but I'd acclimated to the effluvia—inured to the manure, as it were. The fresh air of Wardenclyffe had spoiled me.

I'd grown unused to crowds as well. Two miles of slipping past suited men in bowlers and boaters, denim-clad workers, and long-skirted women exhausted me. How quickly this former Town Mouse had become a Country Mouse.

As always, women's fashion baffled me. Their bustles and voluminous petticoats were bad enough, but their corseted waists looked so uncomfortable, so tight I wondered how they breathed. The hems of their skirts brushed the offal beneath their shoes as they crossed the streets. Why did they put up with it—sacrificing their quotidian comfort at the altar of fashion?

The sight of them reinforced my conviction that my choice to live as a man had been the right one. Had I settled for a woman's life, one day would find me standing in the middle of a busy thoroughfare screaming at the top of my lungs as I ripped off the ridiculous clothing I'd been forced to wear.

At 23rd Street the Second Avenue El left its eponymous route and ran overhead with a thunderous roar, all the way down to East Houston where it made a westward turn. As First Avenue crossed Houston, it changed its name to Allen Street and much of the signage changed to Hebrew. The store windows were filled with brass fittings and such, and the tenement-lined streets became clogged with pushcarts selling everything from dresses to fish to meats to produce. Crossing Delancey Street I was nearly run over by a freight wagon rushing toward the newly opened Williamsburg Bridge.

Finally I reached Drexler's street and was surprised to find it looked like the rest of the Lower East Side. I don't know what I'd been expecting—some sort of oasis of greenery and finery among the tenement squalor, perhaps. I simply could not see a man who drove a Cadillac touring car living in one of these shabby tenements. Many of the buildings were not numbered. As I walked along, wondering how I'd find him, I came upon the answer.

As a child I'd played a game at school called "Which Doesn't Belong and Why?" Here was a building that very much didn't belong.

There in the middle of the tenement block squatted a massive, ancient-looking three-story edifice of stone block. It sat unattached on its property, not deigning to touch its unkempt, red-brick-fronted neighbors. A narrow alley ran along its east flank, and on the west a wider opening, big enough to admit a delivery wagon—or a touring car, perhaps? With its deeply recessed windows and solid granite walls, the place looked like a bank...or a fortress.

A heavy inlaid door sat atop wide granite steps. The Septimus sigil above it convinced me I'd reached my destination.

This had to be Drexler's base of operations while he was visiting the States; perhaps he lived here as well.

I walked up the steps and rapped on the door. After knocking a second time with no answer, I pushed it open and stepped into a cavernous marble foyer. A wide set of steps on the right ascended to the upper floors. And directly ahead, a ten-foot Septimus sigil loomed over the foyer. Just in case, I supposed, someone might forget who owned the building.

To my left I saw what might have been a receptionist's kiosk, but no one was manning it.

I doffed my derby and called, "Hello?"

My voice echoed off the marble walls and ceiling, but no one responded. I did, however, detect a murmur of voices from down the hallway to my right. I followed it until I came upon a large meeting room with some sort of reception in progress. Perhaps fifty men filled the room. A buffet had been set up along the far wall, with piles of food and bottles of Champagne in buckets of ice.

Obviously I'd intruded on some sort of celebration and was about to back out when I realized that I might very well find Drexler here. I'd come all this way looking. No sense in turning back now.

Hat in hand, I stepped inside and began to wander about. I thought I detected Drexler's voice amid the hubbub, more toward the rear of the room. I was headed in that direction when I came upon a large map spread across two joined tables.

A map of the world, laid out in the standard Mercator projection, but the likes of which I had never seen. The lines of longitude and latitude were gone, replaced by...by what I had no idea. Instead the map was crisscrossed by lines that undulated and curved this way and that, made sharp-angled changes of direction, intersecting repeatedly in some places and avoiding others entirely. It appeared as if a child had been given a black pen and told to scribble lines every which way he pleased.

One of the places where multiple lines intersected had been circled in red. I leaned closer and felt an unaccountable chill when I saw they intersected along the North Shore of Long Island—right where Wardenclyffe sat.

"Fascinating, isn't it?" said a voice at my shoulder and I confess I jumped, nearly knocking into the man's Champagne coupe.

"Very sorry," I said. "You startled me."

"No harm done. A little slosh but no spillage to speak of." He thrust out a hand. "William Stubbs. San Francisco Lodge."

Stubbs sported an enviably thick mustache and looked to be about thirty. He'd mentioned a San Francisco Lodge…I supposed that meant Septimus had buildings like this all over.

"Charles Atkinson," I said as we shook.

"You're local?"

"From Britain, actually."

"The London Lodge! I catch your accent now." I offered no denial as he smiled and sipped from the saucerlike bowl of his glass. I gathered from his eyes that this was neither his first nor second serving of bubbly. "You don't look old enough to be a member."

Damn my bloody hairless baby face—again. I decided to lay the Mancunian accent on thick to distract him from my features.

"Here now, I may be new to all this, but I'm a bloody sight older than I look. Came all the way over from Blighty to meet Mister Drexler."

I'd decided to stick to the truth—or a convenient version of it—as best I could.

"Ah, yes! The man of the hour. I noticed you poring over the nexus map as if you've never seen it before."

"Well, I haven't."

"No?" Another sip. "I gather your lodge's loremaster hasn't gotten around to it yet."

"Bloody well hasn't. What are all these lines? They've got no rhyme or reason. They're positively daft."

Stubbs grinned. "It seems that way, doesn't it. But there's method in the madness. They're lines of force called *dlap* lines."

"What force? Electrical force?"

"We don't know. Nobody knows. We don't know exactly who discovered dlap lines or how he traced them—the secret of doing that has been long lost, I'm told—but the pattern of the lines was copied from an ancient compendium in ancient times and passed down through the ages."

I bit back a laugh. "How can that be possible? We didn't discover this bloody continent till the fifteenth century."

"No, my friend. When I say ancient, I mean *ancient*. Before Babylon and Mesopotamia and all that. The First Age. They knew damn near *everything* in the First Age." I saw a hint of suspicion spark in his eyes. "You've heard of the First Age, haven't you?"

Time for a lie. "Of course." And a diversion: "I see these places here and there around the world where a whole gang of the lines converge. What's that mean?"

"Those are weak points in the Veil. Dlap lines point to places where the Veil is thin."

"The Veil?" The word popped out before I could stop it.

Stubbs tensed, suddenly radiating suspicion. "Wait a minute—are you telling me you've never heard of the Veil?"

I forced a sharp little laugh as my brain made a quick correlation. "Oh, you mean the *Wall*! In Blighty we call it 'the Wall.'"

He visibly relaxed. "Oh. Really? I guess that makes sense. It's sort of like Hadrian's Wall when you come down to it. Serving the same purpose in a way."

Obviously he knew a little about Britain. But I knew more.

"We love walls—dry walls, mortared walls, bricks, blocks. Walls everywhere in Blighty. Hardly any veils, though." I laid it on thick, then tapped the Long Island section of the map. "All these nexus points but only one circled in red. Why's that?"

"That's where Drexler found the chew wasps. That's where they came through."

The obvious question leaped to my lips but I bit it back in time as I realized exactly what he was talking about.

Chew wasps...what a perfect name for those abominations.

"Blimey!" I said, trying to bulge my eyes as if shocked. "He's got the buggers caged, I hope."

"Don't worry. You're safe. They're dead."

He said it with such condescension, as if he wouldn't be pissing his pants if a live one flew at him. I wanted to hit him.

"I'd like to see one of these...chew wasps," I said.

"Right this way."

As he moved away, I paused for another look at the map. I treated it as a circuit diagram—albeit one designed by a madman with no knowledge of electricity—and committed as much as I could to memory. At MIT I'd developed a knack for remembering circuits.

The busiest intersections—what Stubbs had called "nexus points"—appeared randomly distributed. The one at Wardenclyffe, then the next closest in the belly of New Jersey. Another far down the coast in Florida, another in the British Midlands. As I moved quickly across Europe, memorizing, I was struck by the lack of dlap lines over the mountains of Romania, almost as if something had pushed them away. Nexus point in Hiroshima, Japan. Others in the depths of the Pacific, one near Hawaii...

"Coming?" Stubbs said.

With one last look, I dragged myself away and followed as he wove through the crowd. We crossed to the opposite corner where Drexler stood in a dark suit with a rather formal Westminster collar, Champagne coupe in hand, holding court next to his trophies: the remains of the three chew wasps suspended in a tank of pale blue fluid, like bugs trapped in a sapphire.

His free hand held his broom handled pistol, which he pointed at the most intact specimen. "I spotted that thing flying straight at me and heard someone shout, 'Duck!' I shouted back, 'That's no duck!' But I shot it anyway."

This brought an appreciative laugh from all those around him. When it tapered off, he brandished his pistol.

"Good thing I had the Mauser along. Saved my life." He gestured toward the black-draped photograph of the fallen Septimus member on the table beneath the chew wasp display and adopted a more somber tone. "I just wish I had it ready in time to save poor Rourke."

His eyes widened, then narrowed when they met mine. He shoved the pistol into a wooden holster on his belt and stepped toward me.

"Excuse me, gentlemen." He lowered his voice when he reached me. "*Verdammt*, Charles! You don't belong here."

I pointed to the chew wasps. "Neither do they. You said you were bringing them to the museum."

"There's a perfectly good reason for not doing that."

"When did they become your personal trophies?"

"They're not. I'll explain everything when I return to Wardenclyffe. But right now, I'm escorting you out of here. Members only."

I didn't resist or protest. How could I? I was a trespasser.

"Can we stop by the map on the way out?"

His face darkened. "The map? You were looking at the map?"

I had intended to taunt him, mention dlap lines, but his fierce tone warned me not to.

"I passed it searching for you. It looks fascinating."

He looked relieved. "Again: Members only." As we passed into the vestibule he said, "Where is everybody? Someone should be on duty here."

"To keep out riff-raff like me?"

He only shook his head. At the door, he said, "Go back to Wardenclyffe, Charles."

"I have questions."

"Which I will answer when I return."

"I want to know why you lied about taking the…" I didn't want to call them chew wasps…"creatures to the museum. Tesla will too."

"I didn't lie. I decided against it. The museum would want to know where I found them. If I told them, they'd have excavation teams all over Wardenclyffe. We can't have that."

No…we couldn't.

"Good bye, Charles."

The door closed with a solid *thunk*.

I stood atop the stone steps, my head buzzing with what I'd learned—and what I hadn't. That map…Wardenclyffe circled in red.

That's where they came through.

Came through what? The so-called Veil Stubbs mentioned?

It's sort of like Hadrian's Wall when you come down to it. Serving the same purpose in a way.

Hadrian's Wall…bisecting Britain from the North Sea to the Irish Sea, studded with milecastles, often described as the demarcation between barbarism and civilization, to keep the former from invading the latter.

And this Veil…did it keep out the likes of chew wasps and things that made fish leap from the water to their deaths?

My mind rebelled. Preposterous. And yet…I'd been chased by a chew wasp…

I stood there, uncertain of what to do, where I might go other than Wardenclyffe. And then I saw her. The Gypsy woman and her dog, standing at the bottom of the steps. When had she arrived? She hadn't been there a moment ago.

"You have questions?" she said in her thick accent. "I have answers."

She turned and walked off in the opposite direction I had come. I hurried after her and we ended at an urban oasis called Seward Park. The space was loaded with children. They had things to climb and swing on. Watchful mothers crowded the benches.

"We talk here, Charles," she said as she stopped by the iron fence. The dog sat by her feet, keeping watch.

I hid my shock. "You know my name. It's only fair I know yours."

"I am called the Lady."

"That's not a name."

"Is mine. What are your questions?"

Where to begin?

"The map…the Wall or the Veil or whatever it is…nexus points… Wardenclyffe…chew wasps…"

"First thing you must understand is that this is not only realm of existence. Other planes exist. Countless others."

Was she barmy? "That's impossible."

She paused and frowned. "How to explain this so you will understand?"

"I'm not stupid, but I'm not gullible either."

"I am well aware of that." She looked at the dog. The dog blinked. "Ah!" She turned back to me. "You have eaten *mille-feuille*, yes?"

"A Napoleon? Of course."

"Imagine one layer of crème filling as world you know, and neighboring crème as world very much unlike yours, separated only by puff pastry. Now imagine *mille-feuille* with endless number of layers, then imagine it curving and twisting in unimaginable ways, impossible ways that leave each layer touching many others."

Isaac Newton had hinted at something like this in one of his books, but still my mind balked. I didn't want her to stop, however.

"Go on."

"In some places puff pastry is thick and in others is thin. Thin places are—"

"The nexus points," I said. I was getting the picture. "The puff pastry is what they call the Veil or the Wall."

"Excellent. Veil is most common term. Now we arrive at map. First thing you must know is that Septimus map is out of date. It comes from compendium that survived cataclysm that ended the First Age—which I have no time to explain so do not ask. A copy now resides in forgotten shipwreck. But long before it was lost at sea, someone copied map of dlap lines and passed it down the ages through Septimus Order."

"But if it's out of date—"

"Nexus point near Serb's tower has not changed. And as you have seen, his experiments are affecting Veil."

I shook my head in wonder. "It seems so improbable. Out of all the possible places he could have set up, he chose one of these nexus points."

"Oh, was not coincidence. He was, shall we say, *guided*."

"Influenced?" The only one I could think of was George Scherff. "By whom?"

"Better to ask, 'By what?'"

"I beg your pardon?"

"Intrusive entities from other layers of cosmic *mille-feuille* have influenced mankind since earliest days of civilization. Is called the Secret History."

I stared at her. I'd never met a truly paranoid person until now.

And then I remembered the chew wasps…and Rourke's corpse. They'd been real, hadn't they? Perhaps I was the paranoid one here.

"Secret history…" I murmured.

"Many know *what* happened, but few know *why* happened. There is commonly accepted reason in history books. Then there is *real* reason, *hidden* reason, and that is Secret History." She gave me a sad smile. "Do you think you came to Wardenclyffe of your own accord?"

My gut twisted. I sensed where this was going but had to ask: "What do you mean?"

"You too were guided."

"Me? Ridiculous! But why? I'm nobody. I'm—"

"You have qualities that can alter game on this particular board."

Game?

"You expect me to believe this is all a game?"

"Of sorts. One we cannot comprehend. Secret History is shaped by countless intrusions, endless moves and countermoves."

Can a mind break? Mine was about to shatter into countless twitching fragments. So I pushed it all aside for later.

"Let's stick to the here and now, shall we? You told Tesla he was cracking the Wall."

"Same as tearing Veil. I use more concrete term for him. Dlap lines converge at thin or weak points in Veil to shore them up. The Serb's transmissions, the waves he creates within the Earth, are diverting dlap lines and creating breaches that allow Otherness to seep through."

"Otherness?"

"A name humans have given to one of the entities, a malign entity. You saw result of brief brush with Otherness: one man dead, one wounded."

"Drexler saw the result as well, yet he seems to be celebrating."

"He did not lie when he said Septimus wishes to change world."

Yes. He *had* seemed sincere.

"A change that includes chew wasps? Is he insane?"

The woman nodded. "Yes. Quite. Because he and rest believe creating chaos will facilitate return of the being they await."

"Who?"

"They call him the One, and he is something more than a man. They believe that upon his return world will change, and they will be handed reins of power."

"Power over a world full of chew wasps?"

Her smile was more than a little bitter. "They are blind to that. They see only power, control. Do not know that chew wasps are merely mosquitos of the Otherness. You cannot imagine..." Her voice trailed off.

"Imagine what?"

"Better if you do not know. And better they do not know that they wait in vain for the One. He is not coming. He will never come. He is sealed away forever."

My brain was going numb. "But—"

"I have said enough. I tell you all this because I do not want you to abandon Serb."

"I would never—"

"He will be trying—terribly trying—but you must keep in mind that is not his fault. He will be influenced."

"By what?"

"Something came through during your last test. Something came through and stayed."

"Like a chew wasp?"

She shook her head. "Far more dangerous. Your brilliant Serbian friend is full of resonances. The straggler from Otherness will disrupt those resonances…disrupt the resonances of everyone within its sphere of influence, causing them to despair, to lose hope, to lose faith in everything and everyone, including themselves, plunging them into darkness. And so is important you stay close to Serb."

"What about *my* resonance? How can I help him if *I* lose faith in everything?"

She placed a hand on my shoulder and stared into my eyes. "You, my child, have no resonance. You are full of dissonance."

She didn't have to explain. Instantly I knew what she meant. A man trapped in a woman's body. What could be more dissonant than that?

And then it struck me.

"You know?"

"Of course. Born Charlotte with Charles inside. Do not think you can hide these things from your Mother."

Mother? Nonplused, I fumbled for a reply.

"My mum's dead."

"That was birth mother. I am other mother."

"You're not *any* mother to me."

"That is because I am your child."

What? What was she saying?

"I have no child!" I would never have children. "But even if I did, how could you be both?"

"Because I *am*, and you must listen to your Mother—you *will* listen to your Mother. You will return to tower and you will stay as long as Serb stays. Is clear? You must not abandon him to the darkness."

I looked away. "I have my own darkness."

"I know your darkness," she said gently. "But is a different darkness. Is coming from within, from your despair. Do not despair. You will not always be alone. But to see that day you must fight the darkness from without that will seek to seep into Serb. He does not understand the power he wields. He has created a hammer and is smashing the Earth with it. Everything you know will change if you are not there to guide him."

"Guide him? He's the maestro!"

"Then you must find way to rewrite his music."

"How? He has the greatest mind of his generation."

"Yes, but he does not have your dissonance. Look for answer inside you. Use your dissonance, Charles. There lies your advantage. *Use it!*"

With that she turned and began walking away. The dog immediately fell into step beside her.

I started after her. "Wait! You can't go ye—"

Without looking back she gave a little wave with her hand and immediately I became frozen in place, unable to move or even speak. Any other day and I might have gone mad with panic—how could this be happening? But after all the madness of the past week...

I stayed that way until she turned the nearest corner. When I was released, I didn't bother going after her. I knew I'd never catch her.

I found an empty bench in the park and collapsed onto it. Ignoring suspicious looks from some of the mothers who probably thought I was drunk, I stared into space and wondered what had happened to the sane and relatively safe world I'd inhabited until I'd entered Nikola Tesla's orbit.

The irrationality of my own situation—a man should not be born into a woman's body—had made me come to depend on everything else being rational. This was why I loved electricity. It had *rules*! And it *followed* them! I could bend it to my will, but only within the limits of the rules.

Up is up.

Down is down.

A is A.

I wanted rules. I *loved* rules. And because my life broke one of the most basic rules of Creation, I wanted more rules, ever more rules for the rest of the world.

But…if what the Lady with the dog had told me was true—and it certainly jibed with my experiences at Wardenclyffe—then the rules were a sham. A chaotic void waited on the other side of a thin membrane, ready to devour us.

And if the Lady was correct, I stood in its way. Because of the dissonance within me.

I didn't understand how that could make a difference, but I knew I had to return to Wardenclyffe.

Something came through and stayed…

I had to find it, and either kill it or devise a way to send it back.

OCTOBER 12, 1937

"Those were dark years back then," Tesla said. "The darkest of my life. I remember so little of them. I was in a fog."

I did not argue. After the chew wasp incident, he dropped into some sort of fugue state where he appeared to function but also seemed lost.

"What's your first clear memory after the chew wasps?"

"Returning to Wardenclyffe in 1906."

"You were back and forth many times during that interval."

"Yes, but they all blur together. I do remember my patents running out and the news being made public, causing my already dire financial straits to turn catastrophic. I recall trying to raise money for Wardenclyffe and other projects, and I remember people I'd considered friends avoiding me."

And I remembered how he retained his rooms at the Waldorf—he never paid his bills there anyway—but could no longer afford lodgings in Port Jefferson, so he moved into his office at Wardenclyffe when he visited.

Rudolph Drexler kept the plant open but minimally staffed. His brief visits coincided with Tesla's, so he spent little time there. He was not aware of the miasma of malaise that had been slowly infiltrating the place.

One by one and two by two, the locals quit, complaining of a vague malady that sapped their strength and will to work. Drexler replaced them with Septimus members, but they fared no better than the locals, sickening and dragging about until they were replaced. I overheard a few conversations mentioning a rash of suicides involving former Septimus workers.

So Drexler was but a sporadic presence. Even George Scherff had to look for work elsewhere. Without local employees to oversee, Scherff became a vestigial presence whom Drexler stopped paying. He kept paying me, however.

That left me as the only continuous presence at Wardenclyffe—along with the thing that "came through and stayed," if it truly existed. I had seen nothing lurking about. Had it submerged itself in the Sound? Wherever it was, I seemed immune to its influence.

"I shouldn't have moved into Wardenclyffe," Tesla said, giving his head a slow shake. "I arrived after the first of the year with the resolution of closing it down."

"I remember when you told me," I said.

"I was shocked that you agreed. If only I had followed through then instead of waiting."

It had broken my heart to hear he'd given up on a wireless world, but knowing what the Lady had told me, and witnessing the mental and spiritual decline of all who stayed at Wardenclyffe, I knew he'd made the right decision.

"If only you had stayed in Port Jeff instead of Wardenclyffe."

He sighed. "Well, you did your best to warn me, but how could I accept the mad tales you told? I thought you'd taken to the opium pipe."

During the interval between my meeting with the Lady and Tesla's return, the progression of days filled with mundane routine had caused me to begin doubting myself. But then all I needed to do was step back and watch the deterioration of the workers to confirm that something had gone terribly wrong at Wardenclyffe.

"But we both learned the truth first hand, did we not?" I said.

"At a cost of thousands of lives."

I gave his bony shoulder another squeeze. "Stop blaming yourself for that. It wasn't our fault."

"Because it was *mine* alone. I had the power to decide—"

"You were not the cause."

"The fault rests with me. I set it all in motion back in 1901 when the first footing was poured. The warnings appeared once we started powering the tower, but I ignored them. The deaths, the destruction, the suicides, the threat to the very fabric of our existence—I carry that with me everywhere. And I always will. Sometimes I wish I had died in 1905, then 1906 would have turned out different. For everyone. I started with the best intentions but turned it into the worst year of my life."

Of my life too. But I didn't say so.

1906

The Ides of March came and went, and not only had we done nothing to shut down, Tesla had ordered a second generator without telling me. When a freight car pulled up on the siding and began unloading it, I stormed into his office without knocking.

"Are you aware—?"

Drexler, sitting close at Tesla's side, held up a hand and said, "Hush, Charles. We are engaged in something important."

I would not be hushed by this man.

"There's a generator—"

"Please, Charles," Tesla said without looking up. "Let me translate this letter." He turned to Drexler. "What did you say his name was?"

"Gavrilo Princip. He is a twelve-year-old Serb living in the small Bosnian town of Obljaj. Being a Christian, he has had a hard life working as a *kmet* under an oppressive Muslim landlord, a life made harder still under Austrian rule."

Tesla shook his head in dismay. "They still have serfs in Bosnia? Disgraceful."

"He is a very smart young man. The Septimus Order is grooming him for better things—for greatness. We are making plans to move him to Sarajevo where he can blossom into his full potential."

"Why do you do this?"

"Despite what you might hear from some quarters," Drexler said, casting a baleful look my way, "Septimus is a charitable organization. We work on many fronts, doing good works all over the world. This is simply one of the ways we try to change the world for the better. We have hopes that maybe someday Gavrilo will change the world in his own way. Maybe he will not. Some trees bear fruit, others do not. We cannot tell the future, we can only present opportunities for others to change it."

"And he has written you this letter?"

"Yes. I was one of his sponsors before I left for America, and I will be so again once I return. In the meantime he has written to me in Serbian, the only language he knows."

Tesla smiled. "I will be happy to translate for you."

Suppressing a growl of irritation, I stalked out and managed not to slam the door.

Drexler had been worming his way into Tesla's confidence, and this was just his latest ploy. For all anyone knew, Gavrilo Princip was a fiction, a Septimus member who spoke Serbian.

I watched the Septimus workers—the only kind we had now—unload the generator while I waited for an opportunity to speak to Tesla alone. What could he be thinking? He'd started the year determined to shut down the operation, and now he was doubling our generating capacity.

Finally Drexler left the office, folding the letter into his coat pocket as he headed out to his car. I made a beeline to Tesla.

"Another generator?" I said without preamble. "What—?"

And then I realized his eyes were closed. They fluttered open. A bit of kip? In the morning? Tesla was three months from his fiftieth birthday, yet he seemed to have aged more since his return to Wardenclyffe.

"Sorry to wake you," I said.

"It's all right. I'm not sleeping well. I have dreams…"

"About what?"

"I can never remember, but I know they are unpleasant. You want to know about the new generator?"

"Why wasn't I told? And what happened to shutting down?"

"Rudy has convinced me to give it one more try."

So Drexler was "Rudy" now.

I said, "You remember what happened the last time, don't you? And the price Rourke paid?"

"I will never forget, but that was a freak happening. Rudy is going to have Septimus's London lodge set up a test on the coast of Wales."

"A bulb test? Like the ones I did?"

"Yes, but this one will be intercontinental. When that bulb lights they will telegraph us. But not only that, he's going to have his people film it as proof. Don't you see, Charles? With proof like that, when we show it to the world, I will be vindicated. The funding will flow like a river. Worldwide wireless will move from dream to reality."

"But what about the tear in the Veil? I told you what the Lady said."

He waved a dismissive hand. "Rudy calls that a fairy tale."

Hurt stabbed me. "You accept Drexler's word and not mine?"

He rose behind the desk. "No-no-no, Charles. You mustn't take it like that. Have you *seen* this Veil? Have you *seen* a tear?"

"Of course not. But I've seen chew wasps!"

"And so have I. But we have an explanation for that."

"Drexler's ridiculous reanimation theory?"

"Rudy has pointed out that what you've told me is simply hearsay, and I am afraid I have to agree. This wandering, nameless woman has filled your head with wild stories." He held up a shaky fist. "Worldwide wireless, Charles. We must never lose sight of the goal. We will power the world, Charles. The *world!*"

I realized then that Drexler had him completely in his thrall. I wanted to turn and walk out, but the Lady's words rang in my head.

...you will stay as long as Serb stays...you must not abandon him in this time of his need. He does not understand the power he wields...everything you know will change if you are not there to guide him.

Guide him? Someone else had usurped that role.

...you must find a way to rewrite his music...use your dissonance, Charles. There lies your advantage. Use it!

She'd said the answer was inside me. Ducky...just ducky. Because I hadn't the foggiest idea what the bloody hell that meant.

* * *

I left Tesla and walked out back to the tower. I hadn't been out here in a long time. It hadn't changed, still looked skeletal. The original plan had been to sheath the eight sides to give it a more substantial appearance, but the money always seemed better spent on something else.

I used to climb it all the time. The incessant wind off the Sound refreshed me as much as the view inspired me.

I saw one of the Septimus workers standing by the edge of the shaft, his blond hair ruffled by the breeze as he gazed down into the opening. As usual, I didn't know his name. When he glanced up at my approach, his eyes looked sad. I gave him a friendly wave which he ignored. Oh, well. Maybe Drexler had been telling them to avoid me, afraid my "fairy tales" would taint their resolve.

I climbed the ladder all the way to the cupola, then sat on one of the struts. April is not a warm month here in the Northeast and the brisk wind off the Sound cut through my shirt and vest. But I loved the view from on high—up and down the coast, across the water to Connecticut, south across the piney stretches of Long Island. Usually it cleared my head, but not today.

I wanted no part of this transoceanic experiment. Drexler had bought Tesla the extra generator for the test, but I doubted he cared whether the bulb in Wales lit or stayed dark. I was convinced his goal was to rip the Veil asunder.

Events had spiraled out of my control. With or without me, the test would go on. Tesla seemed sapped of the will to resist—or did he even want to resist? Vindication is a powerful motivator. The workers, the Septimus recruits, seemed sapped too. Even Drexler was moving slower than usual, and his customarily erect posture had developed a hint of a slump. The Wardenclyffe miasma was affecting him as well, but compared to the rest, he appeared to be bursting with feverish intensity.

Of course, everything was going his way, wasn't it.

I alone seemed immune to the pervasive pall of ennui. The Lady had predicted that, attributing it to my inner dissonance. And yet...

Not completely immune. I sensed something worming its way inside me at night, targeting my ambient despair, chipping away at my will to go on, whispering of the hopelessness and futility of life...

But I was able to fight it off. The Lady's words helped.

Do not despair...you will not always be alone...

I clung to them and rode them to the dawn.

Off to the west, clouds swooped in, obscuring the sun, changing the wind from chilly to downright cold. Shivering, I started down.

When I reached the ground, I found the same Septimus fellow in the same spot by the shaft, still staring into its depths.

"Is everything all right?" I said.

He looked up at me. If his eyes had been sad before, they were positively tortured now. Without a word, he stepped off the edge.

A very girlish scream escaped me—I was too shocked to control my voice. No one was near enough to hear, however. But unlike me, the worker made no sound—not a word, not a cry. He fell in silence.

I dashed to the edge and looked down. The shaft lights were off, so I could see nothing but shadow below a few dozen feet.

"Hello! Are you all right?"

Idiotic question, I knew. It simply came out. After a 120-foot fall, he'd hardly be able to respond. I flipped the switch to turn on the lights but still couldn't see the bottom. Some of the bulbs at the lower end of the vertical row must have burned out. We hadn't been paying much attention to the shaft in recent months.

I ran inside, calling out that someone had fallen down the shaft and I needed a torch. I received blank looks until I said, "Flashlight!" A Septimus worker found one and accompanied me back to the tower. He looked about my age with medium brown hair parted in the middle.

"Who fell?" he said.

"I don't know his name. He had blond hair."

"Oh, no! Steven."

"A friend?"

"I know him. He hasn't been well lately."

"Ill?"

"He cries a lot."

Together we descended the circular stairway as quickly as safety allowed. The worker called out "Steven!" every few steps, but eventually gave up.

About halfway down I turned on the torch. Before leaving, Scherff had bought two new models. They came equipped with fresh dry-cell batteries and the new tungsten-filament bulbs, but even so, the beam didn't penetrate to the bottom.

"Your name's Charles, isn't it," said my companion.

"Yes. And you are…?"

"Herbert. People call me Herb. You're the strange one who lives upstairs."

The strange one…is that what they called me?

"Yes, I guess that would be me."

"They say you're a mad genius."

"I don't know about the 'genius' part."

"What about the 'mad,' then?"

"Not so long ago I would have disputed that. Now I'm not so sure."

Holding the torch stretched out ahead of me I continued the descent into the inky lower depths. But as we progressed, the darkness seemed to swallow the torch's glow. When we reached the lower light fixtures, I realized the bulbs hadn't burned out. They still glowed within their sconces but gave no illumination. The darkness seemed to be drinking their light.

"Something's wrong here," said my companion. His voice quavered.

Brilliant deduction, I thought, but gave a civil reply. "Most certainly."

The flash beam penetrated only two feet ahead of me before being swallowed. We should have been almost to the bottom by now. I slowed my descent and Herb bumped my back.

"Sorry, Charles," he said. "I…I don't want any more of this."

"I understand." I didn't blame him. Terror nibbled at my will to go on. Something *very* wrong here. "You can go back up."

"I don't want to go back up." His voice sounded strained.

"What *do* you want then?"

"Nothing. Don't want any more of *anything*."

That sounded strange but I didn't turn to look. I'd wait until we reached the floor.

But we didn't reach the floor. When I made to step down to the next tread, my foot found only empty air.

"Stop!" I cried, clutching the handrail in fear that Herb might bump me again and knock me off.

I had an indefinable but unquestionable sense of *emptiness* in the dark beneath me.

I handed the torch back to Herb. "Hold this."

But he didn't take it. I shone it in his face. His eyes had a blank look as he stared out into the featureless black void around us. I knew how he felt. I was glad for the solidity of the handrails and the shaft wall to my right. I clung to those—mentally as well as physically.

Seeing that Herb was going to provide no assistance, I held tight to the handrail with my free hand and carefully dropped into a squat. I extended the torch down past my feet and found only darkness. I was perched on the last tread of the stairway, and yet...

The floor had vanished. Only empty darkness waited below.

Not possible...none of this was possible. I had been down here hundreds of times and the floor had always been as solid as rock, as *hard* as rock. Whenever I'd checked the Tesla coil—

The coil.

Fighting nausea and incipient vertigo, I rose and stretched the torch toward the center of the shaft. Its wan glow reflected off the donut of the toroid, along with the primary and secondary coils. All remained attached to the central pipe, but until now the primary coil had been buried in the floor. I knew because I'd helped bury it. No longer. The floor had vanished.

My reeling mind tried to make sense of it. The central steel pipe had been sunk an extra three hundred feet below the floor, past the aquifer not far below, and deep into the substrata as an anchor. Had the floor and the earth below it crumbled into the aquifer?

But that didn't explain this light-devouring miasma, this darkness that seemed almost alive, almost sentient.

And then something *shifted* in the blackness below…*surged… heaved…flowed…*

I saw nothing, heard nothing, and yet I was overwhelmed by an indefinable and undeniable sense of movement down there. What I had thought an inexplicable void where the floor should have been was not a void at all. Something crouched in the depths here. Something had taken up residence in the nether regions of the shaft, and I teetered on the edge of panic at the prospect of meeting the occupant.

"Let's go," I said, turning to Herb and pointing with the torch. "Up! Out of here!"

He didn't respond.

"Herb, we need to—"

Without a word and without warning, he pushed me. If I hadn't had a grip on the railing I'd have tumbled off that last step. As it was, I swung out over the abyss and almost lost my grip on the torch. I cried out in panic. If he pushed me again—

But Herb wasn't interested in me. He moved onto the last tread, then stepped off into the void. And like Steven before him, he disappeared without a word or a cry or a whimper. Simply…gone.

I pulled myself back onto the stairs and began running—yes, *running*—up the staircase. And as I ran, the Lady's words came back to me.

Something came through and stayed…

Yes. Yes, it had. And I had just found it.

* * *

"You're sure of this?" Tesla said from behind his desk.

Again I was struck by how this Nikola Tesla was not the jaunty, cocky, spirited man I'd met in 1903. He seemed drained, smaller, as if he'd sunk into his chair. I had no idea how to reanimate him.

"As sure as I am standing here, sir."

"You do understand it is impossible for the floor of the shaft to simply vanish. It must be *somewhere*."

"It may well be, sir," I told him. "But it's not down there. I assure you it's not."

"He's right!" Drexler said, bursting into the office. He looked terrible—pale, shaken, sweaty. "There's no floor. It's gone!"

He hadn't believed me, so he'd taken a torch and descended into the shaft to prove me wrong. Obviously he'd proved the opposite.

"Impossible!" Tesla cried.

Drexler slapped a hand on the desk. "The schnapps, maestro! Give me the schnapps!"

Tesla looked confused. "Pardon?"

"I put a bottle of *Himbeergeist* in your bottom drawer—for the day we celebrated our inevitable success. But I need it now."

Tesla found the bottle. Drexler uncorked it and drank directly from its mouth. After two swallows he handed it to me.

"Here. Drink."

"No, I—"

"You look like you need it. Drink."

Indeed I did need it. I usually avoided sprits. I'd nurse an ale to be one of the boys, but I dreaded becoming inebriated and letting something slip that would reveal my secret. I couldn't see how a sip or two of this could hurt, though.

I upended the bottle and swallowed. The clear liquid was both harsh and sweet, with a strong raspberry flavor. Drexler took it back for a third gulp. He offered it to Tesla who shook his head.

I said, "It's more than just the floor vanishing into a void. Something is down there."

"This is true?" Tesla looked to Drexler for confirmation. "You saw—?"

He shook his head. "Nothing but blackness down there, but I could sense it. And worse...I felt...worthless." He shuddered as he raked shaky fingers through his hair. He seemed to be talking more to himself than to us. "I've never felt worthless. I was raised to shape history. I have a mission in life, an important position in the Septimus Order—I *matter*! And yet, down there, I was nothing. *Nothing.* Down there in the dark I saw no reason for living a moment longer.

If I hadn't forced myself to turn and run, I might have joined the other two."

He took another swig of schnapps, then corked the bottle.

Tesla looked to me now. "And you, Charles? You felt the same?"

How to put this?

"Oddly enough, no. I know Herb felt that way. Shortly before he jumped he told me he didn't want 'any more of anything.' I believe that jibes with what Mister Drexler is saying."

"But you felt none of that?" Drexler said, giving me a curious look. I sensed his customary imperiousness creeping back. "No hopelessness?"

"No." I almost added that I was sorry. For some strange reason I felt apologetic, but couldn't say why.

"You're an odd one, Charles."

If you only knew.

The only explanation I could think of was what the Lady had called my "dissonance." The disharmony already within me somehow conferred an immunity to the Occupant's influence. It made a strange sort of sense: How could the Occupant disrupt resonance where none existed?

But I could hardly get into that with these two.

I said, "I think we should focus on whatever moved in down there and how to get rid of it."

Drexler was calming, but his usual unflappable poise seemed to elude him.

"Any suggestions as to how we can bell that particular cat, Charles?"

"Yes. Find a way to send it back to whatever hell it crawled from."

A smirk. "Back through this 'Veil' that old woman told you about?"

I reined in a surge of anger at his charade. He not only knew bloody damn well what I was talking about, he firmly believed in it. But I had to keep calm here.

"Still want to call it a 'fairy tale,' *Herr* Drexler? You didn't seem to think so a moment ago."

I detected a quick flinch but he gave away nothing more.

He straightened and said, "I think we should run the Wales transmission test as soon as possible—and at the maximum combined power of both generators. Whatever is down there, we will fry it like an egg!"

Did he realize what he was saying? After what he'd just seen and felt?

"That could create a huge tear in the Veil!"

"Well, then," he said, "if we don't kill it, we will provide it with a pathway back to, as you said, whatever hell it crawled from." He turned to Tesla. "Is that not right, maestro?"

"We must run the experiment," Tesla said absently. "We must show the world."

His words dismayed me. He'd become fixated on vindicating his theory. I didn't know who or what to blame—Drexler, the Occupant below, or a combination of the two—and I supposed it didn't matter or change the fact that Tesla's world-encompassing vision had funneled down to vindicating Wardenclyffe and its tower. He couldn't see past that.

Yes, he was going to change the world. Not to the utopia of his vision...but to the hell of Drexler's.

That left one person to stop all this. And I hadn't a bloody clue as to how to do it.

* * *

By mid-April all was ready—except for the fog. Tesla and Drexler wanted to use a morning fog here in order to obtain the best evidence in Wales. They'd agreed that filming the test in daylight would head off any accusations of trickery in the dark. The plan was to pick a shady spot over there and insert the bulb fixture's probes into the ground in multiple locations. The five-hour time difference necessitated an early start in Wardenclyffe.

I too was ready. Or so I hoped. I'd volunteered to check all the circuits and wiring, replacing anything that might not stand up to the extra power we were planning to run through it. Which I did.

But while I was shoring up the connections in the instrumentation room, I was secretly building a parallel set of circuitry that would counter the effects of the tower. Or so I fervently hoped.

My plan was based on pure speculation and I hadn't the faintest idea whether it would work.

I'd considered and discarded so many plans—like sabotaging the generators, for instance. But that would prove only a temporary solution. I'd be banished, and they'd fix the generators and everything would return to point A.

I had to do something that would protect the Veil rather than tear it.

Use your dissonance, Charles.

I'd returned to basics: What did the tower do? It created standing waves in the Earth's crust that synchronized natural telluric currents. The Septimus map had showed lines of force converging on the weak points to shore them up. The Lady had indicated that Tesla's standing waves were diverting the dlap lines from the Wardenclyffe nexus, weakening the Veil and allowing access from the other side.

The standing waves were the key…and standing waves were synchronous…creating resonances within the crust. Maybe the key was to create a dissonant wave…counter Tesla's standing wave by propagating a disruptive wave that would draw in the dlap lines and reinforce the Veil.

Listen to yourself, a part of me thought. Dlap lines…the Veil… nexus points. You've completely bought into that old woman's madness. It's become a *folie à deux*.

But another part recognized that as wishful thinking. So convenient to write it all off as madness. But I'd seen the chew wasps, I'd visited the void at the bottom of the shaft, I'd sensed the foulness growing there.

Madness, yes. Madness for certain. But madness that existed in the real world. The one I had to live in.

I was ready to sabotage my hero—or at least give it my bloody damned best try. My parallel circuitry was ready. All we needed was fog.

But I needed one more thing: I needed Tesla away from Wardenclyffe during the test in case he detected my countermeasure.

To that end I made the short walk to the Shoreham train station where the ticket agent also acted as the local telegrapher. I found him slumped in his chair behind the barred window, looking dazed. My knock on his windowsill roused him from his reverie.

"How would a wire message reach here from Abereiddy, Wales?" I said.

He looked at me with dull eyes. "Why would you want to hear from Wales?"

An odd remark.

"Please answer my question."

He sighed. "It would be sent through the transatlantic line to New York City, then routed here. Why do you care?"

"Mister Tesla will be expecting an important message some morning soon."

"Nothing's important, young man," he said with a hang-dog expression. "Nothing matters. Nothing at all."

I realized to my horror that the Occupant's influence had spread far beyond Wardenclyffe. Clearly this clerk had been affected. How many others? How fast was it spreading?

* * *

I awoke with water dripping on my face. The loft was usually stuffy and I often tilted the fanlight atop the window next to my cot to allow fresh air to circulate. Moisture was condensing on the glass and dripping on me...moisture from fog?

I leaped up and saw...nothing.

"Fog!" I shouted. "A thick one."

I'd been sleeping in my clothes. We all were. We had to keep both generators ready to run on a moment's notice, so we took turns during the night stoking their coal fires. Drexler had set up a cot in the library downstairs. I had to shake his shoulder quite a bit before he awoke. As he stumbled after me to the main floor to wake Tesla, the maestro emerged from his office, looking as if he hadn't slept all night.

"Our fog is here," I said. "Shall we begin?"

"Is it worth it?" Tesla said, his tone bleak. "Will anyone really care?"

The Occupant was definitely winning.

"Yes!" I cried. "Remember this date: seven thirty-five A.M. on

April eighteenth. This is the birth of world wireless!"

Or, I thought, this is the end of our world and the birth of another in which we cannot survive.

Surprisingly, it took some coaxing to spur Drexler to action, but soon he and I were stoking the generators. Tesla's plan needed all the power we could supply. As did mine.

When the generators were running at maximum output, we gave the maestro the honor of throwing the switch. I'd recruited Drexler in convincing Tesla to await the confirmation from Wales at the railroad station, insisting he deserved to be the first to know. In his current state he couldn't counter the suggestion, so he'd acquiesced.

With Tesla headed for the station, Drexler and I walked out to look at the tower. The latticework of the base was barely visible in the mist but blue-white flashes lit the shaft from below while bolts of energy pierced the fog above.

"I must confess to some trepidation about this," Drexler said.

The admission shocked me. Sanity at last?

"You?"

A quick nod. "I spoke to Stubbs, the brother from San Francisco. He told me you'd been examining the maps at the Lodge. You know more than you should, so I can be frank with you."

He hesitated, seemingly indecisive as to what to say next, how much to reveal. But I already knew more than he realized. Perhaps more than he himself knew.

"You're going to tell me you've been funding Tesla not for wireless power but because he's tearing the Veil? I've already guessed that."

He looked shocked. "You know?"

"You showed up right after the fish died and the barn disappeared."

He nodded. "Don't forget the caretaker's story. The sum of those incidents alerted the Council as to what was happening here. They sent me to make sure it kept happening. But now…now I think Septimus might be probing dangerous territory."

"But the whole basis for your existence is—"

"To prepare the way for the One. But…"

The Lady's words…*they do not know that they wait in vain for the One. He is not coming. He will never come. He is sealed away forever…*

F. PAUL WILSON

Now was not the time to pass that on.

"I saw those chew wasps," he blurted. "And I felt the hopelessness and futility of all existence when I was down in the shaft. In fact, I'm feeling as if this morning's test is all a waste of time. Is that the new epoch my people are working toward?"

I saw a man whose belief system had been built on sand, and was now crumbling. But I didn't yet feel it safe to tell him my plan. I could hint, though.

"We have to seal the Veil."

"Not till we kill whatever is down there or we send it back."

"The Occupant," I said.

"Is that what you call it?" He shrugged. "As good a name as any. It doesn't belong here." He stared at the flashes lighting the mouth of the shaft. "The Occupant cannot be feeling comfortable right now."

"How do we know it feels anything?" I said, starting toward the tower. "I have to go look."

"I wouldn't—"

"I have to see."

Drexler fell into step beside me. "I think I do too. But does it matter what we see?"

It seemed everything was becoming increasingly futile to Drexler.

I, on the other hand, was bursting with purpose. But I needed time before I initiated my counter waves.

We crossed the hundred feet to the base, ducked through the latticework, and inched up to the edge of the shaft. We stood there, tense, uncertain, the flashes from below lighting our features.

I fought a fear—certainly not unfounded—that the Occupant would send up snakelike tendrils and snare us like Timothy Herring up the road. Holding my breath I chanced a quick look, thrusting my head forward and pulling it back almost immediately.

"What did you see?" Drexler said.

"Nothing. A medusa's head of electrical bolts but little else."

The afterimages drifted through my vision. I took a second look, this time squinting to protect my eyes. Again the flashes, but this time I saw the Tesla coil that was creating them. And below it...only blackness. The floor was still gone.

121

Drexler took a turn at peeking, but didn't recoil. Instead, he began leaning farther and farther over until I grabbed his shirt and pulled him back.

"*Nein-nein,*" he said, leaning toward the shaft. "I am fine. I know where I belong. I—"

I pulled him farther away this time.

"Drexler, no!"

He looked at me with terror in his eyes. "Get me away from here."

My thought exactly. But as I was leading him, something the size of a large lobster rose on dragonfly wings from the depths of the shaft. I recognized it immediately.

"Chew wasp!"

Fear overcame Drexler's crushing despair and we ran, but slid to a stop at the braces when we saw what lay between us and the plant. A huge, white fusiform shape undulated along the ground, looking like a fat, thirty-foot maggot.

Instinctively we both ducked at the buzz of oversized wings growing behind us. The chew wasp overshot us and zipped through the latticework, sailing over the maggot thing and banking into a turn for another pass. The maggot lifted its head and shot a gray tendril—its tongue?—at the wasp, snaring it and snapping it back into its mouth. It disappeared without a trace.

…chew wasps are merely mosquitos of the Otherness…

The Lady had been right. But how had she known?

I forgot the question when the maggot angled its glistening body toward us.

"Back the other way!"

The maggot was slow and clumsy and I figured we could exit the base of the tower at the far side and make a run around it to the plant. But the maggot wasn't alone. Through the fog I could see others like it undulating on all sides of the tower, moving toward it.

"Climb!"

I had to get back inside to execute my countermove, but the only way to safety now was up.

As we climbed, something strange occurred—if *strange* still had meaning here. The fog disappeared. Not as if we'd ascended above a misty layer into clear air. No, the fog disappeared, above and below.

As did the plant.

And the Long Island Sound.

All gone.

Replaced by a nightmare landscape under a dark, purple-tinted sky where stars glinted in unfamiliar configurations. With no Big Dipper, I couldn't find Polaris, if it even existed here. A huge, partially fragmented moon hovered just above a horizon that seemed too far away.

Above us, the cupola still blasted blinding, high-voltage bolts of electricity deep into the night; but below...the ground below us crawled with life—the giant maggot things we'd seen, and huge, dark entities that rippled along the ground on massive pseudopods. Chew wasps flitted about, but other things hovered in the air as well, things that looked like man-o'-war jellyfish, trailing tentacles that wrapped up small creatures scuttling along the ground.

It struck me then that I was seeing another world, another level of existence, another layer of the infinite Napoleon the Lady had described. And more, I was accepting it instead of denying it. My view of existence, my *Weltanshauung*, as Drexler might say, had been turned upside down and inside out.

The simple dualism of the Christianity I'd been raised in lay crushed to dust at my feet. God above, Satan below, and humans between—such a nice orderly universe. The kindly bearded Heavenly Father was there to watch over us, and give us refuge from the Devil below. But now...

No one was in charge. Which didn't mean no one was out there. The void wasn't empty, and the best I could expect was indifference. But I sensed no indifference in the reality Drexler and I were observing at the moment. Here dwelled relentless hungers and countless gnashing teeth.

And behind all that, if the Lady could be believed—and she hadn't steered me wrong yet—an endless game in progress, in which we were just another token on an infinite board.

I was looking at the future...the future for all humanity if I didn't get back to the plant.

"This is what Septimus wants?" I whispered, afraid something might hear.

"No," Drexler said. "No one wants this. Septimus has eons of tradition, but I see now it is all…all lies. We have been duped. And we have been *fools*! I should go back and tell them."

"Will they listen?"

"Of course not. A futile gesture. I probably shouldn't bother. But I must. I have a son. I cannot let Ernst be subjected to this nightmare!"

"Then help me get back to the plant. I need to try new circuitry. I did some rewiring without anyone knowing."

"I thought you seemed unusually busy of late. What will it do?"

"Make all this go away."

Or not.

"You'll most likely fail, but we'll try anyway." He started down the ladder. "*Schnell!*"

"Do you have that gun on you?"

"Of course."

"We may need it.

Suddenly we were engulfed in fog—a good sign, I hoped. As we continued the descent I began to make out the lights of the plant. The maggot thing had moved on, giving us a clear path to the rear door.

Drexler landed first, I right after him. As soon as my feet hit the concrete pad I pushed him toward the plant.

"Run!"

He started, but slowed. I passed him and looked back to find him staring at the mouth of the shaft.

"Something's happening," he said.

He was right. The flashes within the shaft had gone dark. Either the coil down there had failed or—

I shouted, "Get away from there!"

Without warning the shaft vomited a silent geyser of blackness. It had no shape. It seemed solid and yet it seemed mist.

The Occupant was loose.

I grabbed Drexler's arm. "Come!"

He shook me off. I couldn't wait for him. I dashed for the supports, climbed through the lattice, and looked back.

Apparently the message that he had to get away finally penetrated Drexler. He turned and dashed after me. He was ducking through the latticework when the darkness caught him, encircled him, lifted him. He screamed, not in pain but in abject terror.

I started back toward him but he was already too high for me to reach. The Occupant was flowing up the tower, slowly but inexorably engulfing each leg and strut as it moved. It had no shape of its own but was assuming the shape of the tower.

Drexler rose with it but became wedged against a truss some forty feet above the ground. His upper torso was free and he had his pistol out, waving it around.

"Go!" he shouted. "Go inside! Do it!"

I ran. I could not reach Drexler, but if my plan succeeded, the Occupant would return to its home, leaving Drexler free.

Wary of chew wasps or worse, I slipped into the instrumentation room and began throwing my hidden switches. When all was ready, I gripped the lever that would reverse the polarity of the Tesla coils—both the one attached to the pipe where the floor used to be, and the bigger one in the tower's cupola. I had no idea if it would work. But it had to. This was all we had.

I slammed the lever home.

The lights dimmed, the generators whined, and then the whole plant began to shake. The reversed polarity and my own circuitry to create dissonant waves of varying amplitude should have started by now. Once they did—*if* they did—Tesla's standing waves would be disrupted. Or not.

I ran back to the rear door, grabbing the fire ax along the way. I hoped I wouldn't need a weapon, but just in case...

The Occupant had engulfed the tower all the way to the cupola but shied away from the flashing bolts. Drexler was still bound beyond reach.

"Is it working?" he screamed when he saw me.

"I don't know. I can't tell yet." I felt so helpless just standing there watching him.

He brandished the pistol. "I would shoot the *verdammt* thing but I don't know where!"

True enough. It seemed without mass and yet it had lifted him and trapped him against the struts and trusses.

At that moment I thought I caught a glimpse of the latticework through the Occupant, but then it was gone. I kept staring and saw it again. This time it remained visible.

"Something's happening!" I shouted.

"What?" Drexler wailed. "Please tell me it is something good!"

"I think the Occupant is fading...fading away."

Drexler began sobbing with relief. "Please make it so!"

"Yes! It's most certainly fading!"

Had my dissonant waves done it? Was the Veil closing and drawing these monstrosities back to the other side?

I looked up at Drexler and saw to my horror that he too was fading.

"*Direkthilfe?*" he cried, his voice full of panic. "*Was passiert? Ich kann dich nicht sehen!*"

I saw what was left of him raise the pistol to his head as he disappeared.

"*Ich werde nicht dorthin gehen!*"

I flinched at the sound of the shot, and then I began to sob. For years I'd loathed the man, but...

Rudolph Drexler had done evil in his life, I was sure, and evils he'd put in motion would keep developing after his death. Once the lust for power took hold, very few got free. He'd been duped, just like the rest of his group, but toward the end he'd wanted to make things right.

The bolts arcing from atop the tower suddenly dimmed. They still flashed but nowhere near as brightly. I smelled something burning and turned to see smoke billowing out the door behind me.

I ran inside and found the source: one of the generators had burned out. I saw no open flames but that might change at any moment, what with the coal fire burning within. I was about to run for a hose when the second generator screeched to a halt and began pouring smoke into the air.

I watched for flames within the billows but saw none. Luck was with us. They'd merely burned out when they might have exploded.

For a while I was the sole occupant of Wardenclyffe.

And then Tesla returned. He came through the front entrance, waving at the dissipating smoke with the telegram in his hand.

"What...what has happened here?" he said as he stared at the steaming ruins of the generators. His eyes seemed more alive than they had in weeks.

Where to begin? So much to tell...the rending of the Veil, the infiltration from the other side, the emergence of the Occupant, Drexler's death...

My brain resorted to the most mundane: "The news from Wales? Good?"

"You mean, did the bulb light?" he said. "Of course it did. Was there ever any doubt?"

"No, sir. None at all."

I hadn't expected glee, but at least satisfaction. Here was the vindication he'd sought. And yet he looked positively unsettled. I sensed something other than the loss of a pair of generators was disturbing him.

"Is something wrong, sir?"

"A news wire came through as I was waiting. From San Francisco. The city is in ruins and aflame after a major earthquake. Thousands are feared dead."

"That's terrible."

"It happened during our test." He looked at me with haunted eyes. "I caused that earthquake, Charles."

TESLA'S MILLION DOLLAR FOLLY

There everything seemed left as for a day—chairs, desks, and papers in businesslike array. The great wheels seemed only awaiting Monday life. But the magic word has not been spoken, and the spell still rests on the great plant.

—Export American Industries

OCTOBER 12, 1937

"You must stop blaming yourself for San Francisco," I said. "There's no possible way—"

"I created standing waves in the Earth's crust," he said, staring off into space. "The San Andreas fault is notoriously unstable. I pushed it over the edge. The result was three thousand deaths."

"As you said: 'notoriously unstable.' The quake was inevitable."

"But maybe not so severe without me."

I sighed. "We avoided far worse. San Francisco lost neighborhoods…we could have lost the whole world."

"That is why no one must ever build another tower, or see the original circuits!"

As we'd stood by the ruins of the generators, I'd explained what had happened to Drexler and the Occupant. I could see the maestro had trouble accepting my story, but Drexler was indeed gone and I had the only explanation.

Then I confessed to my betrayal—how I'd disrupted his standing waves. Instead of being angry, he'd embraced me and thanked me.

Tesla decided then and there to shut down Wardenclyffe. We lit a fire in a trash can out back and began burning papers. I went to the instrumentation room and tore out all of Tesla's wiring. But left my own—the dissonance circuits that would disrupt standing waves. Anyone trying to duplicate Tesla's technology using those would be bitterly disappointed.

The next day we used Drexler's car to drive back to the city. I dropped Tesla off at the Waldorf, then parked Drexler's car, silver-headed cane and all, behind the Septimus lodge downtown. We agreed never to see each other again.

I never saw the Lady again. Coincidentally, however, another woman with a dog was responsible for my meeting the woman who would love me unconditionally for who I am, who would become my wife. Life can be wonderfully strange at times.

Tesla gestured broadly at the city beyond our little park. "You saved the world, Charles."

"Oh, I don't know—"

"No, it is true. I wish I could tell the world about you, but the world cannot know about the Veil and how it can be torn. All that must remain secret."

"Let's hope it will. For a number of years an obscure writer was publishing tales that sounded like he knew about the Veil and what lies beyond it."

"How could he know?"

"A lot of his stories were influenced by dreams. He was just a teen in Providence during the Wardenclyffe years. Perhaps he was sensitive to the breach—Providence wasn't that far from the tower. Whatever, he was a relative unknown who published only in the pulps and died earlier this year. I can't see any way his work will be remembered."

"I am sorry for him," Tesla said, "but the world is better off with all that remaining secret."

Secret…I remembered the Lady talking about the Secret History, and I guessed Tesla and I had become part of it.

He shook his head sadly. "On one fateful morning in 1906, you saved the world while I destroyed San Francisco."

"How do we know my dissonant waves weren't the cause?" The question haunted me at times.

"The standing waves," he said, slowly shaking his head. "My standing waves…"

"Enough of this sort of talk," I said, rising. "Come. I'll buy you dinner."

"No-no-no. We must not. I am being watched."

Despite his previous warning, I glanced around but saw no one. "Surely—"

"Right now this can be written off as a chance meeting in a park," he said. "But if we are seen supping together, they will make a connection and you will suffer."

"'They'? Who do you mean?"

"The government. And Drexler's people. They want my secrets. And I am so afraid they will find where I have them hidden." He looked up at me with an agony of despair. "That taxi accident. Not an accident. I stepped out in front of it, hoping I would die."

"No!"

This poor man. Had the maestro gone truly mad?

"Yet still I live."

He used his cane to push himself to his feet.

"You are the only one I trust, Charles. If I call you, will you come?"

I had no idea what he was talking about but how could I refuse?

"Of course."

He began limping away.

I started after him. "Here. I'll walk you back."

"No! We've been seen enough together. We must never see each other again. Not until I call you."

Five years and three months passed before I received that call.

JANUARY 8, 1943

The maid was being stubborn.

"You see?" she said, pointing to the sign hanging on the doorknob. "It says 'Do Not Disturb.' So I do not disturb."

The call had come yesterday morning.

"*Come to my room,*" the voice had said without preamble. I recognized the accent immediately. "*You must get here first. Bring a briefcase. Do not stop at the desk. Room three-three-two-seven. Leave now.*"

I'd left as soon as I could but snow along the route had slowed my train, and I didn't arrive until mid-afternoon today. I thought I might be too late to be "first," but the sign on the door gave me hope.

So now I stood on the thirty-third floor of the Hotel New Yorker, arguing with a maid.

"He's not answering," I said, knocking on the door again. "I'm afraid something's wrong. You must let me in. What if he dies while we're arguing?"

That spurred her to action. She picked a key from her ring and opened the door. I rushed into the two-room suite ahead of her. She gave out a small cry when we found Tesla lying fully clothed in repose on his bed. As she rushed out, I touched one of the hands folded on his chest and found it cold. He'd been dead awhile.

Strangely, I experienced no grief. He'd had eighty-six years, as full of accomplishment as they were frustration; he'd known riches and poverty, world-changing success and crushing failures. A life well lived. Everything except the love of a woman. But that had been his free choice.

...you must get here first...

Why?

I didn't have to look far. On the nightstand between the bed and the wall lay a stack of papers beneath a white envelope inscribed with *Charles*. I shoved them all into the briefcase I'd brought along and hurried out.

In the lobby I found a seat against a wall, equidistant from the elevators and the front desk, and settled in to watch.

On my way in from Chicago, I hadn't known exactly what to expect. I'd guessed I wouldn't find Tesla alive. But was the call the result of a premonition or premeditation? From the positioning of his body I assumed that he'd died by his own hand. He'd already tried death by taxi. Now, death by...what?

I opened the envelope. Inside I found a multi-page, handwritten letter and an empty medication packet labeled *Digitalis*. I recognized it as a heart medication, but knew no more about it than that. I assumed, though, since he'd given it to me, that he wanted me to know he'd chosen the time, place, and means of his passing via a deliberate overdose.

A middle-aged man carrying a doctor's black bag entered and was escorted into an elevator. I watched the floor indicator stop at *33*. Two men in three-piece suits entered and said "FBI" as they showed identification to the desk man. They too ascended to the thirty-third floor.

I returned to the letter, a very personal message stating how much he'd enjoyed working with me, and how I should not waste my time in the employ of a municipal utility, but break free and find my true potential.

I glanced up and almost cried out when I saw Rudolph Drexler stroll into the lobby. Of course it had to be the son he'd mentioned. Ernst. But the resemblance was remarkable—right down to the silver-headed, rhino hide cane. What was a German national doing here in New York during wartime? He sidled to the side and stood watching.

The two FBI men returned to the lobby and put their heads together. I couldn't follow their low conversation but "OAP" was mentioned more than once. As a naturalized citizen, I knew the acronym: the Office of Alien Property.

I could see where this was headed: OAP would seize all of Tesla's papers wherever they might be, and various government scientists would cull through them for anything of value. I didn't have to sift through my briefcase to know that right now anything of true value was sitting here on my lap.

Drexler must have realized that as a German he would not be allowed within a mile of Tesla's papers. He slipped out as quietly as he had arrived.

His departure sparked a sudden urge in me to do the same. I stuffed the letter into my suit jacket pocket and made my exit.

Outside I stopped on the cold corner of Eighth Avenue and Thirty-Fourth Street. How different the city from my last visit. The streets bustled. Gone were the desperate men seeking work. They were either in the army or laboring in the armament factories. Nothing like a year of global warfare to save politicians from disastrous economic decisions.

Penn Station lay directly ahead. My train back to Chicago would leave from there, but I had time to kill. To my left, the Empire State Building beckoned. On my previous trip I'd had no time to visit the Tallest Building in the World, but I could remedy that now.

* * *

The way the wind buffets the windows makes me glad the 102nd floor observation deck is enclosed. Chicago may be the Windy City but I doubt street-level gusts can compare to a winter gale a quarter mile up. The sun is low enough and red enough now that I can stare into its eye without wincing. The views in all directions steal my breath.

I finished Tesla's letter while waiting in line for an elevator to the deck. Among other things, he told me he burned the film of the successful test in Wales. He ended by repeating what he'd said five years ago:

You saved the world, Charles. The world should be told so it can accept you as its hero.

Saved the world? That April morning seems like a bad dream now, but I suppose I did. As for the world accepting me as its hero, however...I cannot see that happening. The world is a long way from accepting someone like me.

Even though I was able to accomplish what I did only because I am the way I am, that would not be enough. Truly, had I been a woman through and through, and pretending to be a man merely to land the job, I would have fallen into the same funk of hopelessness and despair that affected everyone else at Wardenclyffe. I might even have followed the others in a plunge down that bottomless shaft. Instead, the dissonance roiling within inured me to the Occupant's influence and allowed me to function at a more normal level.

But that would not be enough to prevent my being shunned as a freak instead of lauded a hero. Always I seem to have something to fear. The spread of the eugenics movement throughout the 1920s was frightening enough, but its adoption as state policy by the Nazis is downright terrifying. If they win this war, I and others like me are doomed.

But I remain optimistic. The Allies will prevail.

And here, with the world spread out before me, I know I am not unique. There are others like me out there, many living as demimondaines. Someday the world will understand us, but I have no hope of that in my time. Someday medical science will allow someone like me to be as male on the outside as he is on the inside, but I will never live to see it.

And so my choices are limited. But I refuse to live in the shadows. I have no choice in being an unconventional man, but I can and do choose to live a conventional life, in plain sight…as a man.

And to that end, it is time to return to the two people who matter most in that life: my wife and child.

THE SECRET HISTORY OF THE WORLD

The preponderance of my work deals with a history of the world that remains undiscovered, unexplored, and unknown to most of humanity. Some of this secret history has been revealed in the Adversary Cycle, some in the Repairman Jack novels, and bits and pieces in other, seemingly unconnected works. Taken together, even these millions of words barely scratch the surface of what has been going on behind the scenes, hidden from the workaday world. I've listed them below in chronological order. (NB: "Year Zero" is the end of civilization as we know it; "Year Zero Minus One" is the year preceding it, etc.)

THE PAST

"Demonsong" (prehistory)
"The Compendium of Srem" (1498)
"Wardenclyffe" (1903-1906)
"Aryans and Absinthe"** (1923-1924)
Black Wind (1926-1945)
The Keep (1941)
Reborn (February-March 1968)
"Dat Tay Vao"*** (March 1968)
Jack: Secret Histories (1983)
Jack: Secret Circles (1983)
Jack: Secret Vengeance (1983)
"Faces"* (1988)
Cold City (1990)
Dark City (1991)
Fear City (1993)

YEAR ZERO MINUS THREE

Sibs (February)
The Tomb (summer)
"The Barrens"* (ends in September)
"A Day in the Life"* (October)
"The Long Way Home"+
Legacies (December)

YEAR ZERO MINUS TWO

"Interlude at Duane's"*** (April)
Conspiracies (April) (includes "Home Repairs"+)
All the Rage (May) (includes "The Last Rakosh"+)
Hosts (June)
The Haunted Air (August)
Gateways (September)
Crisscross (November)
Infernal (December)

YEAR ZERO MINUS ONE
Harbingers (January)
"Infernal Night"++ (with Heather Graham)
Bloodline (April)
The Fifth Harmonic (April)
Panacea (April)
The God Gene (May)
By the Sword (May)
Ground Zero (July)
The Touch (ends in August)
The Void Protocol (September)
T*he Peabody-Ozymandias Traveling Circus & Oddity Emporium* (ends in September)
"Tenants"*

YEAR ZERO
"Pelts"*
Reprisal (ends in February)
Fatal Error (February) (includes "The Wringer"+)
The Dark at the End (March)
Nightworld (May)

* available in *The Barrens and Others*
** available in *Aftershock and Others*
*** available in the 2009 reissue of *The Touch*
+ available in *Quick Fixes Tales of Repairman Jack*
++ available in *Face Off*

F. PAUL WILSON is the award-winning, *NY Times* bestselling author of fifty-plus books and dozens of short stories spanning sf, horror, medical thrillers, adventure, and virtually everything between. More than 9 million copies of his books are in print in the US and his work has been translated into 24 languages. He also has written for the stage, screen, and interactive media.

He is best known for his urban mercenary, Repairman Jack. He was voted Grand Master by the World Horror Convention and received Lifetime Achievement Awards from the Horror Writers of America, the Libertarian Futurist Society, and the RT Booklovers Convention. His works have received the Stoker Award, the Porgie Award, the Prometheus and Prometheus Hall of Fame Awards, the Pioneer Award, and the prestigious Inkpot Award from San Diego ComiCon. He is listed in the 50th anniversary edition of *Who's Who in America*.

CPSIA information can be obtained
at www.ICGtesting.com
Printed in the USA
LVHW112334040119
602856LV00001B/38/P

9 781947 654594